# ❧ *The Magic Touch* ☙

## <u>Fiction Series</u>
## The Alex Evercrest Series
The River Front
The Girl on The Grill
Missing
Maggot
Racist
Votive Candles
Windy City
Country Road
Pool of Blood
Sins of the Daughter
Body Parts
The Skull Collector
The Vanishing
The Shadow Fighter
Moonshine
Grief's Trajectory
The Magic Touch
Northern Lights
Alex Evercrest Heroine
Alex Evercrest Collection Two
New Direction
A Family Affair
Disruption
The St. Lebuinnus Church Murder

## A Brian O'Neil Novel
Hawaiian Phoenix
Moon Curser
Death Broker

## The Problem Solver Series
Solutions
Drug Lords
Border Crosser
The Problem Solver Collection

## <u>The Taelo Series</u>
Taelo: The Early Years
Taelo: The Golden Feather
Taelo: Journey of Discovery
Taelo: Dangerous Passage
Taelo: Condor Clan Slingers
Taelo: Circumvention
Taelo: The Journey of Sages
Taelo: Collection
Taelo: Future Leaders Journey

## <u>A Taelo Story:</u>
White Swan and Quiet Pheasant
The Child's Name
Floating Cloud
Quiet Rabbit
Busy Bee
Little Otter & Talking Wren
Broken Spear
Burley Bear & Meadow Flower
Taelo Story Collection

## <u>Science Fiction</u>

**The Savitar Series:**
Journey's End
Savitar
Confluence
Savitar Series Collection

**The Door Series**
The Door
Aliens We
The Endless Hole
The Swarm
Esoteric Journey
The Gentle Eye
The Door Series Collection

**Bram Nielson Series**
The Fold
The Message
Fold Wormhole
Negative Fold
Ripples in Time
Bram Nielson Collection

**<u>Single Science Fiction Books:</u>**
Current Past and Future
The Event
The Door
Viajante 7

# ❧ *The Magic Touch* ☙

## By: *Ron Mueller*

Around the World Publishing LLC
Cincinnati, Ohio

*Ron Mueller*



ISBN 13: 978-1-68223-964-3

Distributed by Ingram
Cover Picture by: Pi03@ShutterStock
Dental Office Picture by: Roman Fenton@ShutterStock
Cover Design by: Ron Mueller

*Ron Mueller*

# *The Magic Touch*

## *1 The Office*

Chase looked out to the lake from the bedroom window. The early morning sun made the rippling surface of the lake throw up sparkles as if the lake was bubbling in golden waters.  He looked across the bed at Amelia and was amazed that after so many years she still looked the same as when they had first met at the medical school.  She had remained single and enjoyed the company of many wealthy men that she had met in Chicago where she lived.  He and Amelia were into each other physically and were friends who over the years had continued to have periodic trysts.  They never went to the same place twice and this time they were in the Finger Lakes area of Pennsylvania staying in a boutique hotel.  They had been enjoying doing a little fishing, some hiking but mostly staying in and enjoying each other.

Today he would be going back to Cincinnati to his loving wife and two kids.  He loved his kids.  His wife was a great facilitator of their social life.  They thought he was attending a dentist retreat focused on dental implant techniques.

He smiled as he thought about the fact that it was half right, he had talked business with Amelia who was one of his partners in his dental implant money "enhancement" program and he was a dentist at a retreat.

He thought back on how he had arrived at this point in his career. He had graduated from dental school, attended specialty training in doing implants, worked for a few years in someone else's practiced and then the opportunity to take over the practice of a retiring dentist surfaced.

Having his own practice was when he had started to make some decent money, but it had taken some innovative steps to start making good to great money. Amelia, who worked for an insurance company in the role of approving insurance reimbursements was one of the key players that had aided that transition. Her handling of the claims from his office allowed him to make claims that were higher than the normal compensation and getting them consistently approved for reimbursement.

It was his tax season and after returning home from his "Dental Convention," Chase focused on getting the paperwork for his taxes prepared. He leaned back in his chair, turned his chair away from the computer and looked out the window. It was after ten in the evening and the yard lighting illuminated the drive up the long hill from the road to the house. He could just make out the roses that at this time of night appeared as black blooms in the circular rose garden at the center of circular driveway.

The perimeter lighting on his putting green just to the left of the window made the flag planted in the hole seem to be signaling someone in the dark. His nearest neighbor was a least half a mile away and he smiled at his imagination.

He looked back to the computer screen directly in front of him. He hated tax season. He had chosen his tax year to end in June. This kept his tax preparer from being bogged down by the taxes of the common people and able to focus on his account only. He kept the information the accountant worked with simple and "clean."

He personally thought that the taxes were far too high, the deductions he was able to generate and to claim was never as much as he wanted them to be. He had no intentions of making large contributions to any charity to reduce his taxes. He wanted all the money he generated to go into his own pocket. He found it easier to adjust his income and to redirect his cash flow out of the country to make his taxes amount to what he felt it should be.

He was making sure all the numbers that he was submitting in his dental office's income and expense form was what his accountant asked for and that it all added up the way he desired.

His recent tryst with Amelia was listed in his computer as a business meeting to discuss the proper way to submit claim forms. He never let his accountant see any of the details of which he was unsure. He did not want an outsider to know too much.

He figured he should be pleased that his dental practice was making a fortune and even after taxes he was well into the top one percent of income in the country. This was only the reported money. What went offshore was almost ten times what his office cash flow amounted to.

As a dentist with a well populated practice, he would have made good money without doing much else, but he wanted more than just a good income. He wanted much more, and he had found a way of getting what he wanted.

Making a fortune was possible because he had two friends in the right places.

One supplying inexpensive implants and one supplying unquestioned expense approval.

Amelia had gone to work for an insurance company and was in charge of accepting insurance claims. She personally managed the claims from his practice. She didn't have to do anything illegal. She just had to authorize full payment for the claims his practice sent in. The expense claims always claimed the highest charges that he could make. He smiled when he thought about the fact that he had a good imagination and his patients all had special needs that cost a significant amount. They were never charged the amount that he claimed so they were not alarmed about the costs he claimed. They paid twenty percent of the bills they saw.

She had her Chicago social circle that included powerful people that ran the lucrative drug trade. He was not sure what her involvement was in that social circle and had no intensions of finding out. He made it a point not to meet her in Chicago. He did not need to get entangled in that trade or with the people she associated with. He was sure that she was providing some sort of service that was also enriching her.

He was happily married, had two kids, and lived in the most exclusive village just to the east of Cincinnati. His wife was from one of the areas old wealthy families. She provided the social connections that allowed him to rub shoulders with the area elite. She also handled the kids and made sure they were in the best schools. She seemed to be clueless as to his personal dealings and he made sure to keep it that way. What made it a good association was that she had her own wealth which kept them from having money issues.

Their kids were both ready to graduate from high school in the next two years. They were bound for college. He hoped they would get a scholarship, but they had agreed that they would make sure that the kids did not end up in debt because of the cost of tuition. Paying for their tuition was no issue and represented only a drip in the bucket of the money he was generating.

The second person that made his scheme work was one of his buddies, Paul, who he had met when he was going to school to specialize in dental implants. He had gone to work for a supplier of dental implants.

He was the source of implants that cost a fraction of what the top-quality implants cost. The implants he supplied were made of less expensive materials and were imported from Guatemala or they were rejects from manufactures of the top implant producers. In both cases he figured that they would last long enough that if they failed the failure could always be blamed on time and some inappropriate action by the person that had the implant.

He just needed the implants to be impossible to trace back to their source.

The billing paperwork Paul sent in for insurance reimbursement was ten times more than what they actually cost to purchase.

The three of them, Amelia, Paul, and he had agreed to split the money that they made equally. This had made all three of them wealthy, able to afford many luxuries and had bonded them together.

Every tax season he shared his accounting numbers with them. It was the one time of the year that they met in person. They would agree to the location, meet there and then spent a couple of days splurging and enjoying themselves. They would spend time enjoying drinks by the pool of some top end hotel, do a little gambling if that was available and partake of the top meals.

Amelia spent one night with each of them. She said she did so because they were sharing everything equally and she thought she should too.

It had been ten wonderful years of getting together. Ten years where each of their fortunes went up by millions of dollars.

This year they were to meet in Miami. He was looking forward to relaxing on the beach and taking in the view of all the young ladies strutting by.

He focused back on the numbers in the spreadsheet showing on the computer screen. He did not want some accountant finding any chinks in the way he inflated the cost of the implants. The paperwork he submitted always supported the numbers and there was nothing for the accountant to question.

Paul provided an invoice for the inflated cost of the implant. This kept his office accounts simple and clean. Even if someone reviewed the paperwork, there was nothing to find.

This also meant that Amelia did not have anything to hide as she evaluated the insurance claims his office submitted to her insurance company. The only thing she did was to accept the claim as submitted. Her participation meant that a smooth cash flow was maintained.

The money from the insurance company was clean. He split the money, so the overcharge went equally to each of the three offshore accounts in their names.

They could each draw from them as needed to support the needs of the lifestyles each of them enjoyed. Each of them enjoyed a superior lifestyle based on the money that was generated.

The reimbursement to his office went into the office's bank account and it matched what the accountant submitted in the tax paperwork.

He ran through the numbers in the income and expense report one more time. It was lengthy but clean. His accountant would be able to use it to generate all the tax forms and determine the taxes he would pay.

The next day he went to the office to interview a new desk clerk. His business was growing thanks to the personal advertising that Luna, the person who ran the office, had started doing on her own. He liked the fact that she had taken that approach on her own. He chose to reward her by giving her another good raise. He figured having another office worker to whom he paid the minimum wage would most likely pay off within the year.

She would be the second hire in one year. His first hire, Ezra, seemed to be working out well. He was a hard worker and handled the orders for the implant materials very efficiently. Next to Luna, he was the one that seemed to work the hardest.

Just as she did every morning, Luna parked her car, took a minute to unhook her phone from the charger and then put it in her purse. She was always the first to arrive, unlock the office and turn on all the lights. She knew that this was not something she got paid to do but she did it out of years of habit.

Once she got to the reception desk, she turned on the two computers. One was for logging the patients in and the other was for scheduling appointments as the patient was leaving. She had ended up with two computers when Dr. Mazerly, the dentist that had owned the practice when she first started, had brought in the second one from his home when he had bought a new computer for himself. She was glad that it was a one Dr. office. She had worked for Dr. Mazerly until he retired and sold his practice to Dr. Thornfield. Dr. Thornfield had slowly increased the number of patients, and the number of dental assistants. Two computers finally started to make more sense.

He had hired Zia and Fiona, dental hygienists who she suspected were lesbians, but she was not sure. She was sure that they had moved in together, went to lunch together and often held hands as they walked to their car. She knew each had their own car because they seemed to take turns driving

She figured that she should just ask them but that would take all the fun at wondering and watching. They did a great job and patients liked them and that was all that mattered.

The most recent hire was Ezra Nightshade, a dental assistant that specialized in dental implants. He was a quiet individual that was very organized and efficient. Most of the time he ordered and organized the tooth implants, the ordering of the crowns and other implant materials. He was a serious individual who focused on doing a good job. He was focused on his work, kept everything organized and was helpful. She liked that.

She not only handled the patients, but at first, she had also managed any office improvements that Dr. Thornfield decided to make. She had almost quit because she felt overwhelmed. When she mentioned that to him, he apologized, gave her a raise, and said that she should hire a contractor to manage the details of the improvements and she focus on managing the contractor.

Both the raise and how he then seemed to check with her with what he wanted to do with the office made her feel she had some say and had some control.

He had added the job of billing and payment to her role so at the end of each month she once again seemed to hit a limit.

She took it on herself to assign setting up appointments of the outgoing patients to each of the dental assistants. At first, they resisted but she showed them how it would actually work in their favor because they could do that as they were winding down while the patient was still in the dental chair.

Ezra was the newest of the group, but he had helped her often enough that she liked him the best. Whenever he was free, he would asked how he could help.

Emma and Bella would get together when they did not have a patient and chat with each other but seldom came to the front desk to see if there was something to do.

As the number of regular customers increased, her job started to overwhelm her once again. This time she went to Dr. Thornfield and suggested that they hire another front desk person.

After a half dozen interviews, she was able to make a hire recommendation and he had hired that person.

Afterwards she felt that the office seemed to be running smoothly and that nothing more exciting was on the horizon.

## *2 The Victim*

Darcy was kneeling working on her flower bed in front of her house.  She had tried her hand at creating a colorful flower bed with a mix of flowers that would attract honeybees and hummingbirds.  She felt great about the fact that she had been successful in attracting both.  She was not sure she would win any awards for the design of the flower choices and arrangement, but she loved what she had accomplished.

She felt that her choices had added both color and made the flower bed seem to be an extension of a flowery meadow.  She had a wide variety of flowers such as the lavender Bee Balm, the black eyed Susans, the blue borage which had a cucumber-like taste that she liked, the California poppies, the violet chives, the lavender Liatris that the bees seemed to love, the bright orange Marigold, and the purple, white, and yellow blooming pansy, the Lavendar which she used to cook into shortbread cookies.

She smiled as she thought about the fact that she visited her flower bed to get some of its rich rewards as much as the bees and the hummingbirds. It provided her a connection to nature that delighted her.

This morning, she was feeling the painful effect of having a new dental implant. She went into the house to look at it in the bathroom mirror.

She leaned in toward her the mirror. She pressed lightly with her index finger on the implant tooth that she had just recently had put in. It looked fine but something was not right. The pain was not too bad, but it was constant. She had arranged for an appointment later in the day to have it looked at. This was her second implant. The first one, which was a back molar, had given her no problem.

Her clear dark brown eyes looked at the wrinkle on each side of her mouth. She smiled and took in the few wrinkles due to the fact that she was always smiling.

"Who could complain about a smile wrinkle," she thought.

There were a few wrinkles on the corner of her eyes that also appeared with the smile, but she thought they gave her character.

She brushed back her long hair that was now almost all grey with a few strands of black hair that created random streaks. She had accepted the loss of her beautiful black hair and had refused to dye it. She was proud to accept age for what it was. It was what it was, and she was aging gracefully and painlessly except for her new front tooth.

She was pleased that her slim brown eyebrows were still the same color they had always been. She thought that they provided a contrast to her hair, and they enhanced her looks.

A makeup minimalist she seldom used lipstick. She felt that her light pink lips were the right contrast to her almond-colored skin. Her parents had both contributed to her olive skin color. Her mother was of southern Italian heritage and her father had been of Spanish heritage.

They both had passed on just two years ago. She missed them dearly but felt that they had lived long, good lives. They had lived out their entire lives on the farm where she had grown up

She turned her head both ways and felt that for a fifty-one-year-old she was still attractive. Her husband always made her feel good when he complimented her on her good looks.

The only thing that was not in as great a shape as she wished were her teeth. On the farm the well water did not have the fluoride that city water had. She had few cavities, but she had several teeth that had deteriorated faster than she had wished.

She had whitened her teeth and felt that had made a big difference as well. She didn't spend money on makeup, but she had spent a small fortune on her teeth. She felt that keeping her teeth in good shape was critical to enjoying her later years.

She drove to the dentist to get her tooth looked at. When she got to the office, the time to get into the dentist chair came faster than she had thought it would.

Ironically, she always feared going to the dentist, but she always enjoyed the comfort of the dentist chair. It made her want to close her eyes and relax.

Dr. Thronfield entered, flashed his brilliant smile, and asked how she was feeling.

She put her finger on her tooth and explained the problem.

He nodded and said he would take a look at it.

He asked his assistant nurse to take a picture of the tooth. He then let her know he would be back shortly to have a look at the Xray.

The assistant, who she had never seen before, introduced himself as Ezra and said that he had been trained as an implant specialist. He asked her to bite down on the shield that would let the picture of her tooth be recorded.

She bit down on the gadget that he put in her mouth and closed her eyes. She heard a buzz and then she was asked to open her mouth.

A few moments later Dr. Thronfield returned and stood with his back to her as he looked at the picture of her tooth. He hummed and hawed a few times and then he turned to her and said that there wasn't anything obviously wrong with the implant. He said that he was going to prescribe a pain killer and said that the pain should subside in a few days.

She nodded but, in her mind, she was thinking that she should say that she actually didn't want the medicine and that the pain indicated to her that there was something wrong with the implant and his response was not what she had expected.

Before leaving the office, she stopped at the desk and made an appointment for two weeks out.

She had no plans to fill the prescription.

Instead, she called a friend and asked her if she had a dentist that she used and felt good enough about, to recommend him. When she got the name, she realized that it was a woman dentist. Once she had the name she called to see if she could get a second opinion about some pain, she was experiencing with a front tooth implant.

She got the appointment for that Friday.

By Friday she was ready. Ready to have the pain come to an end.

She was greeted by a young female dentist who introduced herself as, Dr. Whitlock. She inquired about the pain and then focused on looking at her teeth. After a few moments she asked if she could get a full picture of all of her teeth.

Darcy liked how thorough she was.

After the pictures were taken, she was asked to wait while Dr. Whitlock went to her office where she would take a close look at her entire mouth.

When she came back, she asked if the implant of the molar in the back had been done by a different dentist than the one who had done the front tooth.

Darcy said that it been done by a Dr. Goldens because it had to be done by a specialist.  At that time, she had been a patient of Dr. Mazerly who had sold his practice to Dr. Thronfeld who had recently done the front tooth since he did both general dentistry and implants.

Dr. Whitlock asked if she ever had any adverse effects from the back implant.

She said that she had none.

Dr. Whitlock nodded and said that the material of the front tooth was different from that of the back, and she suspected that the only way to end the pain was to remove the implant and examine it.

She explained that the pain would most likely end immediately on its removal.  She said that she would recommend removing it immediately while she as in the office.  Then a few days later she could put in a new implant.  The same crown could be reused.

Darcy thought for a moment and asked what Dr. Whitlock planned to do with the implant.

Dr. Whitlock said that she planned to send it to get it examined to see what it was made of.

Darcy decided that if the pain was going to end with the removal of the implant, she was ready to do it.

She asked what the procedure would cost and was told that it would be close to two thousand dollars.

She realized that would deplete her entire dental insurance allowance, but she figured it would be worth it if it solved the pain issue.

After the numbing, the extraction was painless. She walked out with a gap in her front teeth.

When she greeted her husband, he asked what had happened to her beautiful smile and what she was sad about.

She explained what had happened.

He said she had done the right thing but that next time she should let him know she was experiencing pain.

She said that she would.

She took it easy for the next week. The pain was gone so she felt that she had done the right thing.

On her next visit to Dr Whitlock's office, she got a new implant put in. It took less than thirty minutes to get the new implant. She learned that it would be three months to allow the implant to be solidly in place. That time was a month longer than Dr. Thronfield had taken.

Dr. Whitlock let her know that the crown was of a lower quality than ones she used but it would do for a short time. She recommended replacing it as well.

Darcy figured that she would let Dr. Whitlock order a new crown.

She commented that she was mad about the situation.

Dr. Whitlock nodded and said that she was also mad, but she was going to wait until she heard back from the expert at the lab she used before she did anything else.  She suspected that the implant material was of inferior quality or not compatible with the human body.

Darcy thanked her and asked if she would take her on as a permanent patient.

That got a smile from Dr. Whitlock who said that she could use more patients and that when they went to the front desk, she would make sure that her receptionist put her on the office patient list.

After leaving the office, Darcy sat in her car thinking about the situation.  She wondered if there was anything illegal about using inferior materials for implants.

She was sure that she wanted to take some sort of action.  The least of the actions was to ask for a refund from Dr. Thronfield.  The other action might be to sue him if he was using inferior implant materials.  But she was not sure if that would be a good use of her time.  She wondered if there were other people that had experienced something similar to her.

## *3 The Snitch*

The creek water rippling down over the smooth flattened water worn stones broadcast the rapid's joyous gurgling that Ezra had listened to all of his life.  It was a melody that soothed his mind.  It was the melody that reinforced his soul.

He had walked this path many times and had been enchanted by the willows bending down to touch their leaves into the clear waters of the stream.  Today he watched as a swallow broke off from its sky flying antics to glide within inches of the water's surface and then dip its beak into the water before rising back to join its frolicking brethren in the sky.

Then his eyes found the finches that were holding onto the branches of the willow picking off what he figured were the aphids and other small insects feeding on the leaves.

He and nature seemed to harmonize.

The swallow had sent him the message of belonging to the group but taking your own action to get the water of life that you needed when you needed it.

The finch told him to hold tight to the branch you had and take action against what was within reach.

He sat down on the large round boulder as he always did every time he made this walk. He looked down into the water and spotted a large catfish slowly opening and closing its mouth as if it was taking slow deep breaths.

He took a slow deep breath of his own.

He put his arms around his knees as he thought about the predicament he faced. He knew what he needed to do, knew he would do it and when he did it, he would lose his job. What bothered him was that he had just started his new job and knew it was not going to look good when he tried to get another job after only a few months. It might not look good, but he knew that would be the way he would go.

He took a deep breath and absorbed the smell of the decomposing grasses at the water's edge, the odor of the pines on the hill sides and the smells of the cattle that pastured just beyond the bend coming down along the creek. This was a bouquet of fragrances that he would never be able to describe to anyone. It had to be experienced sitting where he was. It was what had colored his young life and given him the perspective that the world was made up of the good, the beautiful and the odor of shit that when mixed together was what life was about. This interpretation had guided him in how he handled the life situations that he had so far experienced.

He figured he was still young enough to hold onto his dreams but to realize that dreams tended to change, and they often changed for the better.

He was still looking for love and hoped that someday he would meet the right person. She would need to be independent and be a strong person who was not looking to being kept.

His current issue was what he had stumbled upon at work. He was sure that the Xray he had taken of a patients front tooth implant was a picture of a black-market implant. He had compared it to the implant that was in her record for a back molar and there was a stark difference. There was no way Dr. Thronfield could have missed that fact when he examine the Xray. He was the one that had put it in and unless he was blind the difference in quality should have been apparent at that point.

He was sure there was something rotten in Denmark and that he did not want to be a part of it. How to handle the situation was what he was trying to think through.

He watched as a grey heron landed in the grassy low and marshy area just across from him. It stood frozen for a few moments then in a lightning move its beak went into the shallow water in front of it and came out with a minnow. With a slight flip of his head, it threw the minnow into the air and then swallowed it on its way down.

He figured his job was about to take the same path as the minnow. He was going to get eaten.

He looked down into the water at the catfish and watched as it too made a swift move and a minnow disappeared down its throat.

The lesson for him in both situations was that the little fish always got eaten.

He knew that at the moment he was a little fish.

He smiled as he realized that at the moment nature was not giving him any inspiration to do the right thing.

Then he thought about what he had personally experienced growing up and that he had put into practice for how he lived his life.

In high school he had stood up to the bully and had taken his beating, but he gave the fight his all. He had not won the fight, but the bully had never bothered him again. He was able to walk tall and proud for the rest of the school year.

Then more recently he had refused to participate with a group of dental students that were cheating on tests. They consistently outscored him but on the final test they were caught and kicked out of the program. They lost everything. His score was good enough. He passed, graduated, and got a job.

He had taken the action that each situation had warranted.

Now he would take the right actions, his job would most likely evaporate, and he would once again be looking for a job.

There was one more hurdle that he faced before he was ready to act. He was not sure to whom he was going to report what he had learned.

The boss was the one he was going to rat out and certainly not the one he was going to confront. He needed to determine who to report the situation to.

He turned to see a box turtle moving slowly along the path that he had been walking. He smiled and knew it was giving him the message that he should move slow and steady along the straight and narrow path that he had always walked.

He stood up and stretched his arms over his head and let out a loud shout of "Yes do whats right but do it smart."

He went home and that night as he was watching the news, he saw a young black female detective being questioned by a news crew about her most recent case where she solved a fifty-year-old killing.

It caught his attention because when she smiled, her bright white teeth seemed to be perfect. She exuded a self-confidence and an ease as she spoke that called out to him. He decided that she was the one that he should share his predicament with and ask her advice on how to proceed.

The next day when he got to work, he looked at his schedule and arranged to take a day off. He figured he would visit the detective and would also spend some time looking for his next job.

He called the police station and made an appointment to see her.

He then looked at the want ads for a dentist that might be looking for a dental assistant with a specialty in implants. That did not yield any leads.

On the morning that he was going to see the detective, he stopped at the grocery to get a few items that he needed. As he was getting ready to check out, he ran into Mrs. Barlowe. He asked her how her implant was feeling.

He was surprised when she told him that she had the tooth replaced by another dentist and the pain had immediately gone away. She shared that she also had her crown replaced with a higher quality one.

He asked whether she had the implant and the crown that had been remove. He found out that her new dentist was in the process of having the implant and crown examined.

He let her know that he was looking for a new job because he was on the way to talk to a detective to report what he thought might be an illegal action at his current job and he figured that he was about to get fired. He let her know that it was her implant that he was reporting.

Mrs. Barlowe let him know who her new dentist was and that she had just set up her practice and might be looking for help. She asked him to keep her informed about what he found out because she wanted to take some sort of action.

Once he got to the car, Ezra looked at the time and figured he would swing by to the dentist that Mrs. Barlowe had mentioned.

A short time later, when he walked into the office, he was surprised to see the reception desk empty. He waited a few moments. He heard some conversation just around the corner from the desk and walked back and excused himself.

There was one patient in the chair, and a very good-looking dentist in the examination chair and no one else.

He excused himself and said that he was trying to see a Dr. Whitlock about a job.

She looked at him, asked him to wait a few moments out in the lobby and she would soon be out to talk with him.

He watched as the patient came out to make his next appointment. He noted that Dr. Whitlock was now sitting in the receptionist's chair making the appointment.

He knew that this was a person he would like to know better.

Once the patient left, she turned to him. She apologized and let him know that the receptionist had called in sick, and she was short of dental assistants.

Ezra introduced himself and briefly explained his experience and training. He then said that he had come because he had met Mrs. Barlow who had an implant that had caused her pain. He noticed from the Xray that the implant appeared to be made of a different material from the other implant that she had. He suspected that it was of inferior quality. His training led him to believe that it was a black-market implant that was significantly cheaper than what the normal implant cost.

He asked why she had replaced the implant and what she had done with the implant that she removed.

She let him know that she had sent it off to her lab to get it examined.

He then explained that he was going to meet with the Cincinnati detective unit, specifically with Alex Evercrest to see if his boss's actions warranted investigation.

He added that after meeting with her he was going to return to his current job and quit because he was sure that what was going on in that practice was not ethical.

He was about to ask for a job when a patient walked in, and Dr. Whitlock asked if he could return after lunch.

He asked for her number, walked out to his car, and drove downtown.

On the way he kept thinking about the situation in Dr. Whitlock's office.

He found a parking spot in the garage across the street from the police station and entered into the reception area. He let the receptionist know that he had an appointment with detective Alex Evercrest.

A few moments later he saw her come in. He stood up to shake hands and realized that he was standing a head higher than she. She was accompanied by her partner that was a head taller than himself. After introducing himself and learning her partners name, he followed the two.

Alex guided the person who had identified himself as Ezra into one of the huddle rooms and asked him to share the reason that he wanted to speak to her.

After hearing what he had to say, she let him know that he was potentially on to something, but he was not the injured party and unless he had direct evidence to a crime being committed, he did not have a legal right to complain.

Ezra let her know that he had talked with a Mrs. Barlowe and that she had gone to another dentist that had taken out the implant put in by Dr. Thronfield and had sent it off to get it analyzed. She would soon know if it was a black-market product.

He shared that he was going back to that dentist when he left and would let her know about what he had learned.

He thanked Alex for her guidance and said that he would get the person who was the injured party to come with him next time.

After leaving the police station, he called Dr. Whitlock and asked if he could bring her something for lunch. He liked the fact that she accepted and that she let him know what she preferred from the Chinese carry out that was close to her office.

When he returned to the office, he volunteered to handle the front desk for the rest of the afternoon. He also asked if she would consider hiring him.

He was relieved that she said that she would indeed hire him, but she wanted him to stay at his present job until she had the results about the dental implant.

She went on to explain that if it was a black-market implant, it would add a lot of weight to any accusation that was to be made against Dr. Thronfield if more wronged dental patients were to complain.

She added that she would also bring it up to the State Dental Board as an ethical violation

Ezra agreed to stay on and while they waited for the lab results, he would dig into the transplants that had been done.

He stayed and handle the front desk for Dr. Whitlock for the rest of the afternoon.

During their lunch conversation he had learned that she was single and not dating.

He found it hard to get up the next morning and go in to work.

He was glad that it was Friday.

He called Dr. Whitlock toward the end of the day and asked if she had heard back from the lab.

Then he asked if she would be available for dinner.

## *4 The Situation*

Zia first met Fiona when they both started working for Dr. Thornfield. In only a few days, as they got to know each other, she knew that she was in a complicated situation.

Fiona had married Jason, who had been her childhood friend. When they were young, they had always played house and pretended that they were a happily married couple that had a perfect home. During the year after marrying him she found out that he had a huge temper. They were about to celebrate their one-year anniversary. During that short time, she had witnessed him lose his temper and almost beat people to death. She was the one who always stepped in to stop the fight. Once he was sober, he seemed to return to the Jason she knew. She was questioning whether there was a way for her to back out of their marriage in a way that they could remain friends and not have him loose his temper. Based on what she had learned, she suspected that was not how it was going to work out.

Her ambivalence towards continuing her romantic relationship with Jason was at a height when she met Zia.

At work her relationship with Zia was on a course where the two of them wanted to live together. This was an awaking of what her sexual persona happened to be. She accepted the fact that she had a greater desire to be with Zia than with Jason. This in itself was a surprise to her. She had always felt that there was something missing but had never imagined she was gay. Now that she recognized that fact she felt a relief.

The issue came to a head by accident rather than by a plan. She and Zia were out to lunch when suddenly Jason was looming overhead and loudly accusing her of being a lesbian bitch. It was obvious that he had been drinking because he smelled of alcohol and was very angry. He pulled her out of her chair and slapped her. He was about to hit her with his fist when Zia suddenly gave out a shout and hit him on the side of his head with a swift flick of her fist.

This surprised and stunned Jason who threw her down and turned toward Zia who was less than half his weight and two thirds his size. She took one step back as he stepped forward. She gave out another yell, leaped in the air, and kicked him in the side of his ribs. He grunted and took another step toward Zia.

Zia took a step to the side and then leaped forward as if to embrace him but hit him in the throat with the knuckles of one hand and hit him in the eye with the knuckle of her other hand.

Jason went down gurgling and then fell flat on his face as he passed out.

A policewoman riding a bicycle stopped and asked what had happened.

Fiona explained that her husband had gotten mad, had hit her and Zia had defended her.

She was asked if she wanted to press assault charges.

Fiona declined to do so.

By this time Jason was sitting up and looking around.  He was in shock since he had never lost a fight and losing it to a woman half his size was about as humiliating as it could possibly be.  He stood up and asked if he could leave.

The policewoman warned him about starting fights and said that the next time he would be arrested.

That was the first day that Fiona had gone home with Zia. She was afraid to go home by herself and face Jason.  She did not have Zia's martial arts training.

The next morning, she waited until she was sure that Jason was at work and then she went in, got all her clothes, the few other personal things that were hers and moved them into Zia's apartment.

Since that day she had lived with Zia.  She had found a lawyer, had put in the divorce papers, and had them delivered by a courier.

Jason signed them exactly on what would have been their one-year anniversary and had them returned via mail.

She was happy to have it over.

At work, Luna, the nurse receptionist that ran the office, seemed curious about her and Zia's relationship but never said anything.

The two of them kept things low key.

The office was run out of two separate wings. Regular dentistry went on in the wing she and Zia worked in whereas specialty dentistry went on in the other wing where Ezra worked.

She was surprised at the volume of work that Dr. Thronfield managed to carry.

Things seemed to settled down to a consistent routine, then one day Zia stayed home because she was feeling under the weather.

She went into work and was able to cover the work. Then as she was walking out, she was grabbed from behind and as she was spun around a hard slap made her ears ring.

She had been taking Taekwondo lessons with Zia and she put everything she knew into action. She surprised Jason but he was twice her size, and she was a Taekwondo novice. She held her own as she backed away from him, but she knew that she was losing and was likely to take a beating.

Ezra came out from work and saw what was going on. He gave out a shout and rushed toward the two. He was ready when the person attacking turned towards him. He hit him as hard as he could on the side of the chin and watched as the attacker staggered backward away from him. He was glad to see him turn and run for a pickup parked in the rear of the lot.

He checked to see if Fiona was alright and then pulled her between two cars as that pickup screeched around the end of the parked cars and came towards them.  It did not stop but went charging out of the parking lot.

Fiona thanked Ezra for coming to her aid.

She drove to her apartment and was surprised to be greeted by a police officer as she came out of the elevator.

He asked her if she lived in apartment three fourteen.

Her heart skipped a beat as she said that she did.

He said that her roommate was alive but in intensive care and gave her the hospital that she was in.

Fiona started crying and leaned against the wall.  She asked who had done it.

He said that he was not sure, and the fingerprints found on the small bat that was the weapon was not in the standard police records.

Fiona said she knew who had attacked Zia and she suggested that he check on Jason's car registration for fingerprints and also to check if a black pickup truck had been spotted at the time the attack took place.

She asked if she could leave and go to the hospital.

When she got to the hospital, she found out what room Zia was in and went to that floor and reception desk.

She was greeted by the doctor who introduced himself and said that Zia had come around and had asked if her roommate was alright.  He led her into Zia's room.

She had a large bandage around her head and was hooked up to with a maze of wires on her body.

Fiona held Zia's hand and said she was sorry.

Zia gave a weak smile and asked her if she was the one who had wacked her on the back of her head.

Fionna shook her head and said that she was sure that it was Jason who had done it.

Zia nodded and said that made a weird kind of sense and that he was too afraid of her to face her in a face-to-face fight. She said that she was going to take him on in a legal fight to make sure he ended up behind prison walls where he would find out that his bully behavior would do him no good.

Fionna didn't know what to say. She just held Zia's hand and gave it a squeeze. It was hard not to cry in anger as she looked at Zia's bandaged head. She was sure they had cut off her hair to fix the wound.

She received a call saying that the apartment had been cleared and was now available for her to use. When she asked about the risk, the officer said that a police car would park out front for the evening. They were currently searching for the attacker, but he was not at the address she had provided, and it looked like he had taken all of his possessions with him.

The landlord had let them know that the rent ended at the end of the month and no arrangements had been made to extent the rental.

As she returned to her apartment, Fionna saw the black and white parked out front. She went up to the apartment, prepared a bowl of fruit and took it down to the two men sitting in the car and thanked them for being there. She asked them how she would reach them if her ex showed up. They gave her a number to call and said that if she called that number they would be up within a minute. They said that he would not get past them.

She then went up, locked the door, and leaned a chair under the doorknob.

Jason was up on the roof of a nearby building and had watched the entire time. He had made sure neither he nor his pickup was visible from the air. He lay comfortably under a leaf covered limb of a large old maple tree that reached across the roof as if it was embracing it. It was a warm day, but he had a bottle of water and a bag of sandwiches. He had watched as the ambulance arrived and then shortly afterwards as a person who he figured was Zia was loaded into the back. He was glad it was not a hearse. He wanted her to wake up and go through the pain of recovery and maybe her mental capacity would be reduced. He figured she would think twice about messing with him if they met in the future.

He left the roof and went to the dental office where Fiona worked and planned to do the same to her when she got off work. He figured she would be easy to take down and beat to a pulp. When she came out after work, he grabbed her, spun her around, and slapped her.

He was surprised at the fact that Fionna hit him back and then put up a fight that he was not expecting. She gave him a bloody nose, hit him on the side of the head, and was putting up a good fight until he hit her in the gut. Then just when he thought he would be able finish her off some tough-looking guy attacked him and knocked him back. He was going to return the attack when suddenly he got hit multiple times.

He decided it was time to get away. He turned and rushed back to his pickup. He drove toward the two in hopes of hitting both of them but they both stepped back between two cars. He drove by, shook his fist, gave them the finger, and drove out of the lot.

He returned to the roof near the apartment. He was looking through his binoculars when Fionna brought out what looked like a bowl of grapes and maybe some tangerines to the car where two cops were sitting.

He didn't care about the cops parked out front. He would go in the back, do her in, leave and the two would be out front enjoying their goodies.

He got off the roof, went to his pickup and took out a bat from the bed of the truck. He had decided to make sure that Fiona was put in a hearse, not the back of an ambulance. He walked to the back of the apartment to the door that he had made sure would be open and where he had disabled the cameras. He had a path to the apartment that was all a blind spot.

He got to the apartment door, leaned back and then kicked the door with all his might. He was surprised that the latch did not shatter, and the door swing inward. He stepped back and kicked it again and it still did not move. He cursed his bad luck.

He decided it was time to get out of the building and disappear before the two cops showed up. He ran down the stairs to exit and ran out.

He heard the shout for him to stop. He ran around the corner as a shot rang out. He felt the burn across his shoulder but kept running. He made several turn between buildings as he ran and lost the police. He returned to his truck and took out his emergency kit and worked on the long path that the bullet had taken across his shoulder. It felt like a streak burned across his shoulder.

He was pissed. Somehow, Fiona had blocked the door and had been able to let the cops know he was trying to get in.

He was going to have to get away, but he would have to stay off the highway and get to wherever he planned to hide via the back streets.

His revenge would have to wait for another day, but he would have it and the next time he would kill both of them.

## 5 The Case

After listening to Ezra, Alex asked Johnnie to look into Dr. Thornfield's practice, where he got his implants and where the money went.

She then went to the Chief's office and let him know that she might be bringing in a new case.

He listened and said that if she had several people that had suffered from his dental practice, had obtained legal representation and that law firm asked for help, he would consider opening a case otherwise they should stay away.

Alex walked out of his office and went to her desk.

Trey asked her what she had on her mind. She said that she was going to lunch, and she planned to visit a dentist after lunch.

Trey smiled and asked whether her perfect teeth had a cavity.

She shook her head and said that she had a hunch that she wanted to check out.

After lunch Alex drove to the office of Dr. Whitlock.  She asked the receptionist if there was a chance that she would be able to talk with the doctor.  The receptionist looked at her badge and asked if this was official business.

Alex smiled and replied that in her line of work she was never sure what was official and what wasn't.

A few moments later she and Trey were led to an office in the very corner of the building.

After being asked by the doctor to call her Ava, Alex smiled and said that she had found a person with the same first letter, in her first name, that was shorter than hers.

Ava nodded and said that the only other thing that was short was her height, but it seemed both of them suffered the same fate.

Trey spoke up and said that physical height did not impact the shadow that his partner cast.

Ava smiled and asked how she could help.

Alex asked her about what she had learned about the implants she removed from a Mrs. Barlowe and had sent to the lab for analysis.

"So, Ezra shared that with you," I just got the report back.  The lab found that the material that the implant was made of was of inferior quality.  They suggested that it was a black-market product but had no idea what its source might be.

Alex asked if she knew if Ezra had found a new job.

Ava nodded and said that she had hired him but had asked him to stay on in his current job and do some digging to find out how many patients had received the inferior implants.

Alex shook her head and said that was a dangerous thing to do. If he had names he should quit and leave the office before he was discovered. She had a sleuth that could get into contact with the people on the list and determine the situation.

"That sounds like a great idea. I will call him and get him to quit and come over and work in my practice. Not only do I need someone with his skills, but I need to be able to sleep at night and not worry about him," Ava replied.

She then smiled and said that she was a fan of hers and had watched every news conference in which she had appeared. She went on to say that she would be super confident that something would come from her getting involved.

Alex thanked her for the recognition she was giving her but what she needed was a number of unhappy dental customers willing to put in complaints about the implants that they had received so that the case could be officially opened.

Ava replied that she had one person that was willing to go to court over the matter. She had paid over six thousand dollars for a fake tooth and inferior quality crown.

Alex said that one would be a start and it would open the door but a couple more would bar the door open for a full investigation.

She got the name, phone number for the number the one victim, and thanked Ava for her help. She then reminded her to get Ezra out of the office where he was currently working.

Ava watched Alex walk out and immediately called Ezra and told him to send her all his information and then quit. She shared that she had just talked to Alex who was going to take up the case and had advised her to get him out of the other office.

He replied that though he would love to get out of the office he felt that he needed to stick around to keep track of the situation until an arrest had been made.

He had the information going back to the time Dr. Thornfield had taken over the practice on a thumb drive he wondered what he should do with it.

He got to his car and found it hard to relax. He drove out of the lot and went to the grocery store parking lot. From there he called Ava and let her know that he had all the information with him.

She suggested that he take it to the police station and turn it over to Alex Evercrest before he went home.

He agreed and said that a weird thing had happened and shared the fact that he had been in a fight with someone attacking one of the hygienists. The next day he had found out that the other hygienist was in intensive care in the hospital. He was sure that it had nothing to do with the office but had to do with their personal life. However, he was worried about some sort of revenge by the attacker.

Ava suggested that he come and stay at her house until that situation resolved itself.

He took her up on her offer and thanked her. He asked what he could bring for supper with him.

She gave him her Hopesome home address where she had just moved into a huge granite stone home with a copper roof that was nestled among huge oaks and maples. It was too much home for herself, but she had figured that at the least it was a good investment. It had an over the three-car garage living area that she hoped Ezra would be willing to live in. It would be great to have someone else there to keep things seemingly normal. Besides, she really enjoyed her conversations with him.

Alex was surprised when she came in to work the following morning and found the thumb drive with a note from Ezra saying that he had compiled the names and condition of every implant that Dr. Thronfield had done since he took over the practice from Dr. Mazerly.

She gave the thumb drive to Johnnie and asked him to organize the information so that as they dug into the case, they could trace the source of the implant, the flow of the money and the information about the patient.

Johnnie nodded and said he would set it up like every other investigation they had done.

She then called Ezra to thank him for being so efficient.

She was surprised when he shared the fact that what was on his mind had nothing to do with the fake implants that were being used.

He was concerned about Zia and Fiona, two hygienists, one that was in intensive care and the other who was attacked in the dental office parking lot. He said that he was staying at Dr. Whitlock's home because he was worried about the person who he fought with in the parking lot when he helped Fiona. He was most likely the person who had put Zia in the hospital. He said that he had learned she was hit with a small baseball bat on the back of her head.

Alex asked why he would attack Zia.

Ezra shared the fact that Fiona's ex had attacked her during lunch and Zia had knocked him out using her martial arts skills. It seems that he was able to break into her apartment and was able to hit her from behind.

Alex asked which hospital Zia was in and said that she would check in on the situation. Once she hung up, she looked at Trey and said that they were going to go to visit one of the hygienists that was in intensive care.

Trey shook his head and commented that they were going from simple dental care to intensive care in just one day. He asked what she expected the next step to be.

Trevor and Bill had been listening in. Trevor smiled and said that he had no clue what was going on, but Alex's next steps were always deadly for anyone that was in her way to solving a case. He asked what case they had been assigned to.

Alex smiled and said that the Chief had not assigned anyone to any case.

Trevor asked when she was going to let the Chief know about the case she was working.

Alex bowed her head, said she first had to figure out if there was one case or two and then who should be assigned to each.

Bill smiled said that he wanted the one that did not include any shooting.

Trey stood up and said that he hoped that neither case had any shooting associated with them, but he figured that he and Alex needed to get to the hospital to see how the two cases fit together.

When they arrived at the hospital, they used their police connection to get access to Zia.

Zia gave a brave attempt at a smile and said that she was just realizing that she had almost died. She asked if Jason had been captured.

Alex said that she had just learned about the attack on her and that she was not on the case looking for Jason and had only learned of the situation a short time ago from Ezra.

She asked to hear what she could remember about what had happened.

Zia shook her head slowly and said that she had been dozing on the couch waiting for Fiona to come home. She came awake to Jason shouting at her to wake up and then the world went blank. The next thing she remembered was dialing 911 and telling someone that she needed help. Then she had come awake here. She added that was all she could recall.

Alex let her know that she was going to dig into the situation and would most likely get the case officially opened.

She wished Zia a quick recovery and said that she would be in contact with her and that she should not leave the hospital without giving her a call. She handed her one of her cards that had her number on it.

On the way to the car, she called the Chief and let him know that she wanted to meet with him about the Dental Scam case.

She then called Bill and asked him to get the police report about the attack on Zia. She let him know that she was coming in to talk with the Chief about it and about the case that she had Johnnie doing some preliminary work on.

She called Johnnie and asked him to organize whatever he had been able to dig up in the short time he had been working on the files that Ezra had given them because she was coming in and wanted to have the Chief officially designate it as a case.

She arrived at the station and walked briskly into the bullpen area. Johnnie held up a folder and said that he was ready. Bill held up a folder and said that he was ready.

Alex nodded and walked to the Chief's office and knocked. She went in and a moment later she waved for everyone to enter the office.

The Chief smiled and looked at the group and said he wondered how long it would take for Alex to demand that she be allowed to go after the crooked dentist.

Alex said that she was actually bringing two cases to him. Both were located in the same dental office but one was a con scheme of interesting proportions and the other was about love gone wrong.

The Chief shook his head and asked if anyone in the room was surprised that Alex would bring up such a twist to a case.

Travis said that he did not remember a case that was normal and did not have some unusual twist since Alex had joined the detective unit. Even the last case was not normal because though someone did die, Alex was not the one that did the shooting and that was really abnormal.

Alex thanked Travis for his thoughtful commentary, but she wanted to hear what Johnnie had to share and then she would introduce the second case and have Bill share what he had learned.

Johnnie said that the doctor had been running his scam for more than ten years. During that time, he had been able to generate almost one hundred million dollars that he sent to three different offshore bank accounts. He did not have time to verify if taxes had been paid on that money, but he doubted that it had.

He would be able to verify that angle once the case was opened and he had access to the tax records. He then pointed out that there were only eleven individuals that were no longer patients of Dr. Thronfield and might be convinced to testify against him. One patient was ready to testify against him but there had not been time to identify anyone else and have their position checked out.

Alex looked at the Chief and said that she was relatively confident that one or two more customers would be found to testify against the doctor. She then said that she wanted the case officially opened so the needed work could be done to put the good doctor and whomever was working with him away in prison.

She then asked Bill to share what he had time to learn about how the dental hygienist from that same office ended up in intensive care.

The Chief held up his hand and asked how the second case was connected to the first.

Alex replied that they were linked only because the person who had given them the inside information about the good doctor was also involved in the situation that involved a love triangle gone bad.

The Chief chuckled and said that he was glad that there at least was the thinnest of linkage.

Bill shared the fact that the dental hygienist that was in the hospital had been surprised by her attacker who hit her with a miniature oak baseball bat. She just barely survived but was now on the road to recovery.

Her roommate had been the wife of the attacker but had divorced him and had moved in with Zia. The report stated that her ex had returned that same night to the apartment and tried to break, but a chair propped under the entry door handle prevented him from getting in.

There were two police officers parked out front. One got to the door in just under one minute. The second went around the back of the building, got a shot at the attacker, and managed to wound him but the attacker got away.

Dr. Rogers team was able to get enough of a blood sample to verify that it was Jason Gravely the ex-husband. There is a standing warrant out for his arrest that lists him as armed and dangerous.

Alex looked at the Chief and said that they could work it as one case or two cases, but they needed his blessing to take the cases on.

The Chief ask how she was thinking about the cases.

Alex said that she felt that Bill and Travis should handle the love triangle case. She smiled and added that she was sure that Travis would have a unique insight to love triangles gone wrong.

He laughed and replied that he had been involved in dozens of love triangles during his thirty-five years of marriage.

Travis commented that it was just like her to give him and Bill the case that put people in the hospital and was the most dangerous.

Alex laughed and said that she thought she had heard him earlier say he wanted the case that had some gunfire associated with it. She added that she was concerned that he would be disappointed about her inability to satisfy that desire, so she had given him one that at least had some bloodshed associated with it.

Bill shook his head and said that they should ignore his partners complaints and suggested they focus on the case at hand.

She then said that she and Trey would handle the dental scam case.

She added that Johnnie would be a resource for both cases.

The Chief looked around and asked if the split made sense.

Bill said that it did and that it seemed clear that there were at least three people in danger of the ex-husband.

Johnnie said that he was sure that even without any patients willing to testify, he would be able to provide information to their IRS friends that would put the doctor away for many years.

The Chief nodded and said that they had two cases to solve, and everyone should work together to get them solved. He looked around and said they should get out of his office and get to work.

## *6 The Arrests*

Chase learned about Zia and was disturbed that personal issues might upset his dental practice and might cause it to get investigated. He called Fiona into his office, asked her what was going on and why he should not let both her and Zia go.

Fiona knew that both she and Zia needed their jobs. She pointed out that she was working overtime to make sure that no patient was ignored. She had worked with Luna to make some slight changes to the schedule to make sure she could handle the load on her own. She pointed out that the insurance was covering the hospitalization costs and that it would not interfere with providing the services the patients would request.

Chase thought about the situation for a moment and figured that the office could weather what was going on. He asked if the person who had attacked Zia had been arrested. When he found out that he had not, an alarm bell went off. He could not risk some crazy guy coming into the office and wreaking havoc.

He would need to set up some sort of security. He would get Luna to arrange it.

Fiona left the office knowing that Dr. Thronfield would soon find out that the attacker was her ex and then he would fire both she and Zia. She did not know what they would do then. She hoped that by that time Zia was out of the hospital.

She experienced a real low in her self-confidence. It seemed that everything that could go wrong was going wrong.

Once the case was official, Alex arranged a meeting with Dr. Thronfield's accountant.

Johnnie had done a very detailed analysis of the money flow. He had learned that the money from the insurance company was sent to a specific bank from which the money flowed four ways. One sum flowed back to the dental office and the other money split three ways and went to three separate offshore accounts.

She put in a call to Joe Brown the Cincinnati region IRS leader and asked to meet with him to share a potential case for him to manage.

When he understood the details of the case, he asked if it was illegal to use inferior dental implants.

Alex said that she was not sure about that, but she was sure that the Dr. had not paid taxes on millions of dollars that he had sent to offshore bank accounts and that was what she was going to arrest him on.

She, Trey, Johnnie, and Joe met at the accountants office and asked about Dr. Thronfield's tax records.

The accountant objected to sharing the records until Joe spoke up and said that he had the official IRS paperwork that authorized him to review the records to see if the income of the practice matched what had been submitted as the amount that taxes were paid on.

The records that were shared were in perfect order. Joe made the point that Dr. Thronfield was not to be told of his visit for at least a week. Any sooner and he would arrest him for conspiracy to defraud the government.

When they left the office, Joe verified that Johnnie was sure about the more than one hundred million that had gone offshore. He then said he would get authorization to seize the doctor's personal computers at home and at work as well as any paperwork that might be found at each location. He figured to do a simultaneous raid on the Dr.'s office and his home within a day.

He said that it was clear to him that the operation was sophisticated and most likely needed some outside help for it to work.

He pointed out that someone had to supply the inferior implants and to bill them as if they were top quality ones. He added that there might be someone on the other end from where the money would come. He added that from his experience twenty percent or so would come out of the victims pockets and the other eighty percent or so from the insurance company.

So, the two victimized entities were the patients and the insurance company.

Alex said that she would hunt down the supplier of the implants. She would have Johnnie work out how the money came in and then went to the off shore accounts. He would share this with Joe and his people as a guide for them to gather the in-court materials.

Alex returned to the office and asked Johnnie to identify the outside people that might be involved in the Doctor's implant scam.

Johnnie tracked down the dental implant supplier and learned that it was a person named Paul Elsher. He did a deep dive into Paul's personal finances and his ability to obtain the implants.

He had been expecting to find the implants coming from Asia but instead he found out that the supplier was a small company in Belize. He dug into that business and found out that they produced the implants and shipped them out to various Latin American countries and to a Texas address where Paul lived.

Paul in turn, using a dummy organization, shipped the implants to Dr. Thornfield's office as top-quality implants and charged slightly more than what top quality implants cost on the market.

Alex knew that this information cleared the accountant of any complicity in the scheme. She called Joe and let him know of the situation.

Joe thanked her and said that he would have the Texas regional IRS folks made aware of the situation and get prepared to assist her when she was ready to make her arrest.

She asked Johnnie to check on the insurance reimbursement side to see how Dr. Thornfield could consistently get the reimbursement that he wanted to get.

Johnnie was able to identify an Amelia Lockwood that worked for an insurance company but was also registered as an independent agent that handled all the submittals from Dr. Thornfield's office. She had agreements with the handful of insurance companies that handled dental insurance and all of the claims from his office were personally handled by her.

Alex let the Chief know that once again she was going to be going to Chicago and needed his help in getting her Illinois authorization re-established. She was sure that Lieutenant Governor Jane Stradford would once again give her legal status in her state.

She added that in Texas they could use Randolf Task the IRS agent there to help her when she was investigating Paul Elsher.

Unknown to Alex, she was on a Chicago mafia watch list at the airport. The new mafia boss learned of her arrival shortly after her landing. He had her followed to see what or who she might be investigating. He saw it as a potential opportunity to settle an old score. She was held accountable for eliminating his predecessor and the one before him. He did not intend on getting eliminated. He instead planned take preemptive action and do the eliminating.

The tail that he had assigned to follow her let him know that she had gone to the IRS building and had stayed there for an hour and then she had gone to the location where she and an IRS agent had entered the building.

He knew the address. He had attended several parties there held by his central Chicago area leader at his long-time girlfriend's luxurious penthouse apartment. He had not only enjoyed the party, but he was taken by the lady that he later learned was part of an insurance scam that was paying for her lifestyle. He figured that she must have gotten herself into the spotlight and was being investigated.

He sent up a sniper to a building that provided a good position from which to take a shot with the order to shoot to kill the detective and anyone with her.

Alex and Trey got out of the car, followed Andy Weller, the IRS leader and one of his partners. Johnnie had been able to determine that Amelia worked from home, so they took the elevator to the penthouse floor and rang the doorbell. They were planning to arrest Amelia, seize her computer and all the paperwork associated with her work.

Amelia came to the door and was going to deny them entry until she was handed the legal paperwork authorizing their entry and the seizure of her records. She was shocked when her linkage to the money that she had in her offshore account was disclosed and she was asked if she had paid taxes on it.

She at first denied having the account but when she was handed a picture of her sitting and signing the paperwork when she established the account, she knew she was caught. She had opened the account more than ten years ago and she wondered how the pictures could have been acquired and asked about it.

Alex smiled and said that she had the ability to time travel and get whatever she needed.

Alex led the way into the apartment and suggested they sit down while the IRS team collected all the records in which they were interested.

While they were sitting and watching the computer systems and records being carried out, Alex asked Amelia how long she had known Dr. Thornfield and Paul Elsher.

Amelia smiled and asked how the connection between them had been made. She was sitting and thinking that she would love to make a call to her mafia beau and ask for help. She was smiling but she would love to shoot all three of the persons sitting with her. She had her own gun but there was no way of getting to it otherwise she might shoot them herself. When she was asked to stand up and then had handcuffs put on, the smile left her face and she muttered that they would regret treating her in the manner of a common criminal.

Alex nodded and quietly replied that was what a person in her position was labeled but that she was innocent until proven guilty in a court of law.

Amelia listened as she was read her rights. She was then escorted out of her apartment. The ride down the thirty floors was silent.

They were walking toward the black sedan when suddenly Amelia and the agents were knocked down.

Alex was pushed and then something hit her on her left shoulder. Before she could react, she was lifted by Trey who carried her under his right arm and ran into the alleyway between two buildings. He put her down and asked if she was alright.

She smiled and said that except for the rough handling she felt OK. She put her hand on her shoulder and asked if there was any damage to her jacket or if there was any blood.

Trey nodded and said that she was going to need to replace the jacket because there was a long gash across the shoulder. There was no blood. He commented that the sniper had relied on technology that improved accuracy, but the laser beam made the shot visible. He had spotted the laser and had pushed everyone and then hauled her into cover.

A few moments later the area was a sea of flashing red and blue lights.

Amelia was surprised at what had happened, but she was pleased that her friends had taken action. She decided it was time for her to demand a lawyer and to have all communication with the IRS handled by him. She was also going to have him sue the IRS for the pain of her bloody knee that she had gotten when she was pulled down behind the car when the shot had been fired.

Alex identified herself and Trey as agents with the Illinois Lieutenant Governor's office working with the IRS on a major tax evasion case.

Trey pointed out the most likely building from which a sniper might have taken the shot that had hit his partner.

Alex's jacket and Kevlar jacket were put in an evidence bag.

An EMT took a look at her shoulder to verify that she did not have a flesh wound.

She figured that she would not even have a bruise from the glancing hit. She gave Trey a hug and thanked him for his quick action.

He smiled, said that he was suffering from a sprained shoulder and that she would need to lose a few pounds.

She knew that he was joking but she replied that she was a few pounds over her fighting weight otherwise she would challenge him to a fight.

She checked with the IRS folks and got agreement that they had the case. She reiterated that her team would provide the necessary information that would lead them to an airtight tax evasion case. She then let them know that she and her partner were off to the airport on their way to Texas.

As they were getting on the airplane, Trey asked when she was going after the person who had ordered the hit.

Alex shook her head and said that she was not sure, but she was focused on getting to San Antonio so that she could arrest the third person that was part of the trio that was hoodwinking honest dental customers.

On arrival in San Jose, they were met by Randolf Task the regional IRS agent.  On the way to Paul Elsher's home Alex updated him on the approach she had taken to eliminate the scam of implanting inferior teeth as quickly as possible.

Randolf said that he liked leading with the tax angle and then following up with a civil case suing the doctor for the damages, suffering, and pain.  He made the point that the three that were being arrested would be in prison and they would be easy to find.

Paul heard about the arrest of Amelia from her mafia friend. He had a small fortune of dental implants he wanted to capitalize on.  He was in his garage hurriedly closing down his operation and getting all the implants ready to ship out.  He figured that in a few days he would fly down to his favorite resort in Jamaica and stay there until he figured where in the world he would permanently settle down.

He heard his doorbell ring and froze.  He was not expecting anyone.  He opened the side door of his garage and looked out to four people who were standing outside of the front door.  He picked up the double barrel shotgun he kept by the door.  He stepped out and called out to them to leave his property.

He watched as the tallest of the four at the door stepped forward and held up some paperwork and said that it was a search warrant and that he should put down his shotgun.

He was just pulling back the triggers of the shotgun and lifting the barrel when he looked down at a spot on the white shirt that was turning red.  He continued to pull the two triggers back and then a second spot appeared on the left side of his shirt.  His finger pulled the shotgun's two triggers simultaneously and the shot gun fired into the ground, lifted him into the air and he flew back into the garage.  The world went black.

Alex shook her head and said that he had been stupid, and she had done what she did so that he would not lift the barrel of the double-barreled shotgun up any farther.

Randolf said that he had never seen anyone shoot so fast and accurately.  As he walked toward the garage, he used his gun to point to the foot deep hole the shotgun had blasted into the ground.  His partner had preceded him and said that Paul was dead.  He added, "two to the chest and one between the eyes."

Alex listened as Randolf called in the shooting.  He signaled to the team that had arrived by van and told them to gather all the evidence and put it into the van before the local police arrived so they could leave and get home by dinner.

He walked over to where he saw Alex sitting and talking to her partner. He listened as they joked about the fact that she was ahead on the body count of taking out those who made the mistake of choosing to use their weapons versus their minds.

It was clear to him that the two shared a much more dangerous profession than he.

Alex looked up at Randolf and asked for his people to let her know that they were at the right address and that the person she had just shot was Paul Elsher.

He said that they were at the right address and the van that was backing into the driveway was getting ready to load a ton of fake implants into it. They would also take the computers and all paperwork that they found. He added that his team would be gone in less than three minutes, but he and his field partner would stay until the local police cleared all of them to leave. He let them know that he had called, talked with the local chief of police bringing him up to speed on the situation and had been assured that after any required evidence was collected, they would be allowed to leave but the chief wanted their incident reports in by the end of the following day.

Alex nodded and said that she would have it done by the time she ate desert that evening.

Randolph suggested they go to one of his favorite places for dinner where he would recommend something like Texas Quail, grilled sweet potatoes, stuffed mushrooms, apple slaw and pecan pie for desert. He added that they also had some of his favorite wines.

Alex said that she would take his suggestion and their conversation ended as the local police arrived.

She was now thinking about the steps she was planning to take with the remainder of the case.

## *7 Triangles Don't Always Close*

The hours she was keeping exhausted Fionna. Released from the hospital but still recovering, Zia needed help in getting around. Fionna would make sure Zia had a good breakfast, left a lunch to warm up and then prepared dinner when she got home. The hours added up and the fatigue crept in.

Jason was still on the loose and that worried both of them.

She purchased and installed a steel bar that went across the entrance door in hopes that would prevent Jason from breaking in. She still put a chair under the latch. She had also put a bar in the sliding door that went out to the apartment's small corner porch.

She took note that Dr. Thornfield had hired some security guards and she made sure she arrived to work after they arrived and that she left work before they left. She made it a point of giving them a few pieces of candy each time she met them. Their presence meant that she could at least relax at work.

She had gotten to like Ezra for the fact that he always checked to see how she and Zia were doing. He almost always walked her to her car after work. It was clear to her that he was concerned about the situation.

Jason was working part time at two jobs. He arranged his time so that he could spend time on the roof of the building where he could see the apartment that Fionna and Zia lived. He had also found a place he could park and then walk to where he sat in the bushes and watched the dental office's parking lot. Once he realized that there were armed security guards he stopped sitting in the bushes. He then focused on getting ready to get into the apartment where he planned to kill both of them.

He figured the opportunity to get to both of them had to show itself in the near future. He would be ready and eliminate both of them at the same time. He now had a three-fifty-seven and his slugger baseball bat as the weapons he was planning to use. He planned to use the baseball bat to beat the two to death. The three-fifty-seven was to shoot any police shooting at him when he made his getaway. He hoped to kill the two and leave the building unseen and then leave the state and go somewhere west.

He was very familiar with the sound of the bat hitting a hard ball. He was looking forward to the sound of the bat hitting Fiona solidly in the head. He imagined it would sound like a dry tree limb being broken when the wind ripped it from the tree. He smiled at the thought.

Fionna knew that Jason would fixate on getting even and would be watching her and Zia until an opportunity to attack them seemed to be to his advantage. She was always on full alert when she got home and had to get up to her apartment.

The one consistent activity that she and Zia had participated in was in their martial arts classes. They were both in the same Aikido and Taekwondo classes. Zia was about four belts above her, but she was making progress up the belt sequence faster than Zia. She was determined to hold her own the next time Jason attacked her. She figured that there would be a next time and it would be when she least expected it.

The two of them returned from the session where she had just earned her first-degree black belt. They had celebrated with a T-bone steak dinner, a bake potato smothered in butter and sour cream and four grilled asparagus spears each. They toasted with a glass of a lovely Cabernet Sauvignon that had a hint of the flavor of blackcurrants, mixed with a pepper-like lingering after taste.

They sat down on the couch to read, enjoy their wine and chill.

Suddenly the door and door frame seemed to exploded inwards with pieces of it scattering all around the entry and the kitchen. The chair and the iron bar was meant to keep the door from falling in but the battering ram being used blew through it as if none of it was in its path.

They both threw their glass of wine at Jason as he entered swinging a ball bat. Zia went around the left side of the kitchen island. She went straight for Jason. What was left of the door and the door frame all fell into the apartment toward her.

She watched as Jason dropped the battering ram and took hold of his baseball bat. As he started his swing, she stepped in toward him but still felt the bat hit her ribs. She took hold of the bat with one hand and rolled in backward toward him and hit him in the face with an upward swing of her closed left fist. She realized that Zia had jumped on his back and was trying to twist his head. She pried the thumb of his right hand back and he let go of the bat. He had reached up with his left hand and was trying to pull Zia off his back by her hair. He suddenly pulled his right hand back away from her and hit her on the back of her head with his forehead.

His right hand reemerged with a very large handgun. She pushed back toward his chest and grabbed his right wrist with one hand and put her index finger in with his trigger finger. The first shot went almost straight downward along Jason's leg. He pulled his arm upward as he screamed in pain.

She pointed the gun toward the other side of the living room and kept pulling the trigger. The kick back caused the bullets to walk up the far wall until the gun was empty.

She knew that she was slowly succumbing to the pain in her ribs and that she was close to passing out. She gave a scream and hit him in the throat with all her might and then collapsed.

She felt Jason falling and stepped to the side as he went down with Zia still on his back.

She collapsed against the wall and passed out.

When she came to, she watched as Zia used one of their steak knives to cut a hole in Jason's throat and poke a large bubble tea straw into his windpipe.

The firing of the pistol must have been loud enough that one of the neighbors called 911. Just a few moments later the police arrived in mass.

The EMT's check Jason out and complemented Zia for having acted in time to save Jason's life. They stopped the bleeding from his leg wound and then they strapped him to a board and hauled him out. Then they checked her out and said that they thought she had two broken ribs. They carefully strapped her down, put her in the ambulance, and sent her off to the hospital.

She was not sure whether she passed out, but she came awake in the dark of the night wondering where she was, then she saw Zia sleeping in the chair next to the bed. Jason's attack and her and Zia's actions replayed itself. She reached out and took Zia's left hand in hers and went back to sleep.

When she woke up again Zia was gone, and a note said that she had gone into work and would cover for both of them. She knew that they were barely getting by from paycheck to paycheck and neither of them could afford to be out of work.

The library cart came to her room, and she selected a book to read.

Before she could get into it, an attending doctor came in and let her know that she had three broken ribs that had been totally broken from the rib cage and had fallen into her chest cavity. He let her know that it was a small miracle that she was alive.

The ribs were reattached by screws at the backbone end and the other ends were attached at the sternum by wires to the ribs above and below them. They were now stable, and everything was held in place with a tight wrap that she would have to keep in place for several weeks. He prescribed some pain pills and let her know she should not drive for at least a month after being released from the hospital.

She was just getting ready to open her book when Alex Evercrest, her work partner and a lawyer walked into her room.

After greetings she asked why Alex had come. She listened as Alex introduced John Williams, a lawyer that she had asked to be the prosecutor to represent both her and Zia in court and to prosecute Jason for premeditated attempted murder.

She, Trey, and John had visited the scene and had been amazed that someone had not died.

She learned that the three of them had already stopped by the apartment and taken pictures of the shattered door, the bullet holes in the far wall, and the rest of the mess that had been created during the fight.

She was surprised that they had also interviewed the neighbor that had called in the 911. She was asked to describe the fight.

Alex listened to the description of the door exploding inward and the fight that ensued. She was impressed with the actions that both Fiona and Zia had taken, especially Fiona's firing of the revolver until it was out of ammo. The bullet exit holes could be seen from the ground and were as large as a grapefruit.

John had pointed out the use of the battering ram and commented that the attack was definitely premeditated. He pointed at the bullet trail on the far wall and wondered just how it had been made. As he listened to the story, he knew that it was going to be a case where he would put the attacker away for at least thirty years and most likely for life. He was aware that Jason would be questioned by the police once he could talk. He would remain handcuffed to his bed and guarded that entire time.

Jason awoke to find that he had his right wrist handcuffed to the bed. He used his left hand to feel the bandaged that was taped over his nose. He could feel several bandages on his head as well. His leg was elevated and when he removed the sheet over it, he saw that the bandage ran from just above his knee down to his ankle. He remembered the pain when Fiona had pulled the trigger the first time. He had pulled his arm upward and she had kept pulling the trigger. Then she had finished him with a flick of her wrist. He could tell that he was breathing through a tube in his throat. When he looked at his right hand, he could see that he had a broken thumb.

He wondered how he looked.

The nurse who came in held up a mirror and commented that from what she had learned he was lucky to be alive and that the women he had attacked had done a good job on him and then saved his life.  She added that she hoped that he was feeling as bad as he looked.  She handed him a cup and let him know that he was on a liquid diet and would be given smoothies or soups that he could drink through a straw.

She smiled and wished him a very painful day.

A few moments later several policemen entered and read him his rights and asked him to indicate that he understood what he had been told.  They let him know that he was being held for attempted murder.  They then turned and left.

He looked at the wall and wondered what was in store for him.  He wondered how long he would end up in prison.  All he knew was that what he had planned had blown up in his face.  He had envisioned looking down at two dead women.  He had never envisioned ending up in the hospital in such a battered condition.

At work, Zia had been able to handle the double schedule.  She was exhausted and now knew how Fiona had felt a few weeks back.

Luna and Ezra had been great at helping to manage the patients so that she could handle the load.  Ezra had prepped the patients and chatted with them until she was free from the person before them.  She figured that both she and Fiona should reward his friendship in some way.

She felt the effects of the fight the night before and then sleeping in the hospital chair next to Fiona's bed. She wondered how Fiona's day had been. Fiona had been in surgery for several hours as the doctors reattached her ribs.

She had planned to go to the hospital during lunchtime but had fallen asleep.

She was just getting ready to leave work when a John Williams introduced himself and said that he was on the way back to his office but thought he would stop by to get her version of what happened the night before.

It took her about thirty minutes to share what she remembered had happened. She realized that the entire attack had taken less than four minutes but her telling took three times as long and the attack seemed to have been much longer. It was definitely something that had distracted her for the entire day.

She was relieved to learn that Jason would most likely end up in prison for thirty years and perhaps for life.

Once the interview was over, she decided to go straight to the hospital. She stopped and got two smoothies and two orders of onion rings. She knew these were both Fiona's and her comfort snacks and comfort was what they needed.

It was hard to look ahead, but she felt that once Jason was put away, she and Fiona could safely get on with a life she hoped would be filled with more sunshine than rain.

## 8 *The Root of the Matter*

A lex and Trey were in the Chief's office bringing him up to date with the status of the case. She explained how during the arrest in Chicago a sniper had attempted to kill her, but that Trey had saved her life by pushing her so that the bullet hit her vest and then he had carried her into the alleyway. He had also pushed Amelia Lockwood to safety, and she was suing because she scraped her knee.

The Chief asked if they had determined who had set up the sniper and was that connected with the case.

Alex shook her head and said that she thought the sniper had nothing to do with the case. She figured it was most likely connected with the two previous cases where the mafia heads were killed, and she was blamed for their deaths.

The Chief asked what should be done about the sniper attack.

Alex smiled and said that she planned to chat with the Mafia boss and show him how detrimental killing her would be, but she would wait until the dental case was closed.

The Chief shook his head then asked if he wanted to know what the chat would be about.

Alex said that he probably should stay in the dark about what she would show and tell the mafia head.

The Chief nodded, said he understood and then asked about what happened in San Antonio.

Trey spoke up and said that a two-barrel ten gauge shot gun being raised to shoot had happened.  He described the person they were there to arrest coming out of the garage pulling back the two triggers of a double-barreled shot gun, and then starting to raise it.  Both he and Alex shouted out twice to put the gun down.  When he began to raise it, Alex shot him.  Amazingly the blast of the two barrels launched the shooter back into the garage but he was already dead as he pulled the trigger.

The Chief looked at Alex and asked if there was any other option.

Alex shook her head and said that she was actually a little slow with her reaction because he was able to pull the trigger and the hole blown into the ground was clearly large enough to have killed all four of them.

The fact that they had retrieved close to six hundred inferior quality dental implants and the information of where the implants were made at least verified that they had the right supplier.

She added that he was guilty of participating in the scam and unfortunately had thought he could get away with a deadly threat.

She then said that she was going with Joe, their IRS friend, to arrest Dr. Thronfield right after lunch. She added that the IRS case would close down the operation. She then informed the Chief that she had connected John and Hanna to the victims of his practice, and they would be filing civil cases for injuries. That would potentially mean financial restitution and a ruling of compensation for pain and suffering to the patients. Between the two trials, she figured that the doctor would be out of business and in prison for a long time.

The Chief nodded and asked about the side case that involved the two dental assistants at the same office. After listening to how that was turning out he said that it was amazing that all of that was going on in the same dental office.

Alex smiled, said that she agreed and added that the root of the matter had to do with "love gone wrong, and greed gone strong."

Ezra had participated in three inferior dental implants a day for more than three weeks as he waited for Dr. Thronfield to be arrested. He had talked several times to Ava about the situation and she had coached him to document the situations but to wait until the doctor was arrested.

Toward the end of his wait, he learned that Fiona was in the hospital after Jason broke into her and Zia's apartment. He was relieved to learn from Zia that Fiona was going to recover and that the two of them had put Jason in intensive care where he was recovering but was under arrest and would be facing premeditated murder charges.

During lunch he went with Zia to visit Fiona in the hospital and took a bouquet of flowers to her. He then helped Zia to handle a double workload so that she would not get fired.

Alex led the way into the dental office. She showed her badge to the receptionist and asked to see Dr. Thronfield.

When Dr. Thronfield came out to talk to them, Joe showed him his IRS credentials and let him know that he was under arrest for tax evasion and read him his Miranda rights.

Ezra had watched as the doctor was arrested.

Luna shook her head and asked what she was going to do about the upcoming dental implants and the regular dental customers.

Ezra said that he would recommend contacting Dr. Ava Whitlock to take over the implant cases and ask her if she knew of a dentist that could handle the general dental care cases.

He talked to Alex and let her know that he had documented all the dental implant cases that Dr. Thronfield had done since he had started doing so at this office. He said that there were several cases where the patient had complications.

Alex thanked him for the information and let him know that a lawyer from the practice of Williams & Waverly would be in contact with him and would be requesting it.

Ezra called Dr. Whitlock and let her know about Dr. Thronfield's arrest. He let her know that he was going to have the receptionist, Luna, call her to arrange coverage for the office's dental patients. He then had Luna call.

He listened as Dr. Whitlock agreed to see the implant patients and give them the choice to become her patients.  He also listened as Dr. Whitlock gave Luna the name of a general dentist to take on the other patients.

He felt a huge weight lift off his shoulders as the reality of not having to keep secret the scam that Dr. Thronfield had been practicing.

Luna was shocked by Dr. Thronfield arrest.  She was shocked but not totally surprised.  She had gotten the impression that Ezra knew the details about the arrest and asked him about it.  As she heard the details, she came to realize that the implant part of the practice had been a scam from the time the office had transitioned to Dr. Thronfield's ownership.  She had the details in her records and knew that the IRS was going to want to have all of it.  She also realized that the practice was going to take a hit in the cash it would be generating.

She worked with Dr. Whitlock and got her to agree to keep the current staff paid in the short term and to see how the two offices could be managed as one.

She was pleased with Dr. Whitlock's request for a recommendation for a receptionist for a job at her office.  She asked about the salary and was surprised that it would be more than she was making.  She asked if she could apply for the job and was pleased to know that she could.

Dr. Whitlock was pleased to be picking up a significant number of new dental implant clients. She would offer all of them a free consultation as part of having them move into her practice. She figured that if she also hired Dr. Thronfield's current receptionist the merger of the patients into her current practice would be seamless.

She called a good friend that had graduated a year behind her and asked if she was interested in acquiring a going general dentistry practice. She did not know what the practice would cost to buy but she shared that the current dentist had been arrested for tax evasion and he would most likely be sued for malpractice. It could be a fire sale.

Dr. Thronfield was in a state of shock as he was taken to the IRS office where he was grilled on the details of all the implants that had he had done. It was clear to him that his goose was cooked.

He had amassed almost one hundred million dollars that he held in two offshore accounts. He thought these accounts would be out of the reach of the IRS.

Somehow, they had the details to the accounts and the exact amount of money that he had in each. They even showed him signing the papers when he set up the accounts. He wondered how they had been able to get those.

Then they showed him a picture of Amelia in handcuffs and of Paul being put into a body bag. He lost it and said he was done talking and he wanted a lawyer to represent him.

He needed to figure out the way forward. He asked if he was allowed to leave but was informed that he would be held at least until charged. He would be allowed to call the lawyer of his choice, or he would be assigned a lawyer if he so chose.

He called the office of his long-time lawyer and was referred to one of the partners who specialized in cases dealing with the IRS.

The next day he met with a Lutecia Underway. She asked him if his patients were given a choice in the quality of implants.

He shook his head and let her know that the patients were never aware of what was going on.

She let him know that she would look into the possibility of him being sued by former patients when they were informed about what he had done.

He asked why they would be informed. She explained that he was being taken to court because of tax evasion and the IRS might dig into how he had made so much money. They seemed to be very secure on the case that they had, and she would seek to get the details.

She let him know that he would be going to court the next day to hear the charges against him and then she would have enough information to determine what their next action should be.

He was returned to his cell and issued a change of clothes and led to a shower area where he was told to shower and change into clean clothes.

That evening his wife came to see him. She asked what he was being charged with. He made up a story about there being a misunderstanding and that he would be cleared of any wrongdoing.

He thanked her for bringing in a set of clean clothes for him to wear to court the next day.

She let him know that she would be there, but she was keeping the kids in school and away from the trial. She let him know that he had made the evening news, and the kids knew about his arrest and were wondering what he had done.

The next day he was led to court where his lawyer declared that he was pleading innocent to the charges of tax evasion and money laundering. He was denied bail when the prosecution highlighted that he was a flight risk. He had to give up his passport and would remain in custody during the trial.

After the court session, his lawyer let him know that her office had received a call from a lawyer representing a Dr. Ava Whitlock that was offering to buy his practice.

He thought about it for a moment and figured that selling the practice was most probably a good idea. He would not be able to stay in Cincinnati when the details that would undoubtedly come out during the trial became public. He put the price at two years of practice income as it appeared on the tax record.

Joe called Alex to let her know of the outcome at court and the fact that the detailed information that she had turned over to his team was being followed up on and he would have a very foolproof tax evasion and money laundering case against the doctor.

It would put him in prison for at least ten years.  He said that he felt great about the case, but the good doctor would still have quite a sum of money after paying the taxes and the penalty associated with the delay in paying.

Alex shared the fact that she was working with Hanna Waverly to sue him for the pain and suffering of the patients he defrauded. He would be close to penniless when she got done with him.

Joe chuckled and said that she had made his day and that he would charge ahead with his case.  He asked her what she would be doing now that she had closed the case.

Alex replied that she had some unfinished business in Chicago that she had to deal with before she was ready to go on to the next case.

## *9 Jason's Trial*

Jason's day in court rolled around.  He was still aching from his wounds, his nose was still bandaged, he was now breathing normally but could hardly talk and in general he felt miserable.

Zia and Fiona were sitting just behind the prosecution's table.  They were holding hands.  They had watched Jason being led in wearing an orange jump suit and then sitting down at the defense table.  He still had a bandage over his nose that Fiona had broken and a bandage over one eye that Zia had scratched.  He was charged with premeditated attempted murder and faced a minimum of thirty years to life in prison.

Their personal lives had yet to get into a regular routine.  Fiona was still trying to get over her broken ribs and to not yet able to carry a full workload at the office.  So far by early afternoon the pain in her ribs made it almost impossible for her to continue.  She really appreciated the help that Ezra gave her by taking over for her.

The office went into a few days of turmoil when Dr. Thronfield was arrested. The fear was that the office would close, and they would all be jobless.

She became aware that Ezra had been doing more than being a dental assistant. He seemed to be the central person who had all the information of the scam that the doctor had been practicing. He also seemed to have the connection to another dentist who a short time later took over Dr. Thronfield's business. She had come to the office and interviewed all of them and asked them to continue working at what was now her office. She had let them know that she would not be the one who would do the regular dentistry, and that she was bringing in a friend who was a general dentistry practitioner who would eventually own and run the practice.

She let them know that Ezra would be moving to her office since his specialty was on the implant side of the practice which would be handled entirely out of her office.

Zia squeezed her hand as John Williams, leading the prosecution team stated that he planned to show beyond a shadow of doubt that Jason had planned to kill Fiona and had tried twice to break into her apartment to do so. The first time he had been thwarted by the fact that he could not break into the apartment, and he had to run since the police were at that point still providing protection.

But that on the second time he had come prepared with a battering ram. He pointed to the battering ram and said that it was evidence that he was putting in front of them so that they could realize that Jason had planned his attempt at killing both Fiona and her partner Zia.

He then pointed to the small bat that was laying with the handle on the battering ram. He then pointed to Zia and stated that it had been used against her in revenge and had put her in the hospital. Then he pointed at the large bat. He said that it had been used at the same time that the battering ram had been used to break into the apartment when he went in with the intent of killing both of them. He pointed at Fiona and stated that she was still recovering from three broken ribs that had to be pinned and wired back to the rib cage during surgery.

Zia was called to the stand first. She was asked when she had first encountered Jason. She explained the lunch scene where she had knocked Jason down. She was asked about the fact that she was a mere one hundred five pounds and she had defeated Jason who was twice as large and twice her height. She shared that she was trained in Tae Kwon Do and Akido.

Then she was asked what happened a few days later.

She shared the fact that she had been sleeping on the couch and when she woke up, she was being beaten by something and the next thing she knew she was waking up in the emergency room at the hospital.

She had suffered a concussion and found out later that Jason had broken into the apartment and beaten her with a miniature baseball bat.

John held up the miniature baseball bat and asked her if that was the weapon.

She replied that it was.

He asked her how she could be sure.

She replied that her blood was found on the bat and Jasons fingerprints were also found on the small bat.

She was then asked about the next encounter with Jason.

She replied that happened when she and Fiona were sitting on the couch and reading. The door and door frame imploded inward and the chair that was propped under the door handle broke down. She had jumped on Jason's back while Fiona rushed at him from the front. She added that she could hear Fiona's ribs cracking like wood being broken over one's knee as the bat slammed into Fiona. She was surprised that Fiona was able to step into Jason, deliver a throat punch, and shatter his nose before collapsing. She was still on his back as he collapsed because his Adam's apple had been crushed and he could not breath.

She said that Fiona was laying against the wall when she took a knife and opened up Jason's airpipe and put a large straw into it so he could breath.

Then the place was overrun with police and EMT's.

She was asked what happened next.

She said that the EMT's took Jason out first and complemented her on keeping him alive.

Then they carefully put Fiona on a carrying board so she could not move and took her to the hospital.

She was the only one that got checked over and given a clean bill of health and then she spent several hours as the police took her statement and documented the damage to the apartment.

Fiona was then called to the stand. She was asked why Jason had attacked her the first time. She replied that she had filed for divorce, he had signed the divorce papers but then had wanted to rescind and demanded that she return to him. He slapped her and then Zia knocked him down. He was about to retaliated when a policewoman on a bicycle showed up and sent him on his way.

She was asked when he showed up again and she pointed to the battering ram and said when he came through the door with the battering ram in his hands.

She was then asked what happened next.

She said that she attacked from the front as Zia jumped on his back from the side. The pain from getting hit did not register until she had stepped in, hit him in the throat with her fist and then she had driven upward with the heel of her hand into his nose. After that, her world went blank, and she collapsed. She recovered shortly and watched Zia cut open Jason's throat. At first, she had thought Zia was killing him but then realized that she was providing him a way to breath.

The next thing she remembered was waking up in the recovery room with Zia holding her hand. She was told that she was lucky to be alive because the three ribs had broken loose and were floating on her lungs but had not punctured them or damaged the heart which was just above them. She learned from the doctors that the three ribs were screwed to where they joined the backbone and wired to the good ribs at the other end.

She was asked about the pain and responded that it still hurt her to breath, and she was still required to wear a tight wrap to hold the ribs in place.

Suddenly Jason stood up started to come around the defense table as he shouted that he hoped her ribs would hurt the rest of her life because she had ruined his.

Two policemen pulled him back by the arms and chained both his wrists to the table and his ankles to rings on the floor.

The Judge called for a recess until after lunch.

Alex got a call from John and was informed that the morning session had gone even better than he could have hoped because Jason tried to attack Fiona when she was testifying. They were on a break until after lunch. He was going to deliver is closing arguments and the defense then would have their chance to try and prove Jason's innocence to the charge of premeditated attempted murder.

He said that the jury should be able to reach a quick verdict.

After lunch, the defense said that they would not call any witnesses but that the jury should consider the fact that Jason had never been in trouble with the law and would not benefit from prison time but what he needed was counseling. They should consider finding him guilty of a spontaneous action that deserved some prison time but not as many years as the prosecution was asking.

The judge then called the trial to an end and instructed the jury to go to the deliberation room and determine the guilt or innocence of the accused.

Less than an hour later the jury returned with a guilty on all counts verdict.

Jason put his head down on the table and then began shouting that the two bitches had ruined his life. He tried to pull loose, and he kept shouting that he planned to kill them. He then began pounding his head on the table. He was restrained by two policemen.

The judge said that he was sentencing Jason to sixty years in a maximum-security prison. He would be eligible for parole for good behavior after thirty years.

He then declared the case closed.

# *10 A Friendly Discussion*

*A*lex had spent several weeks thinking about how to handle the Chicago mafia boss who evidently had some sort of vendetta against her. She figured that a surprise visit to his office where she would reveal the extent to which she had the pulse of his business would go a long way to getting him to focus on his illicit business and not on her. She hoped that her ability to have information about his family in Sicily, his cash flow in Chicago and the fact the she could tell him about his offshore accounts would shock him.

She asked Johnnie to use his skills to detail the cash flow of the mafia business in Chicago.

Once he had that detailed, she asked him to located the base of operation in Chicago and find a way to get into the Mafia boss's office without letting anyone in his security group know.

Then she wanted to know all the personal history of him and his family and their financial situation in detail.

Johnnie joked with her that it was going to cost her multiple trays of her cookies for such a huge request.

It didn't take him long to follow the flow of the money. A large amount seemed to go in circles in the Chicago area to pay off his field workers and as bribes to various police officers.

A small percentage went out to Sicily into accounts owned by the Italian mafia dons.

Most of it made its way via several banks to three offshore accounts and then ended up being invested in the stock market where the laundered money made legal income. However, it was income that was not reported, and no taxes were paid on it. Johnnie knew that Alex would want a detailed documentation of those accounts.

Locating the Chicago mafia office was not difficult but figuring out how Alex and Trey could enter and go to Aldo Viscuso, the Mafia Chief's office undetected was much more of a challenge. He worked backwards from Aldo's corner office.

He found a freight elevator that was just thirty feet away from the office. The freight elevator went all the way down into the basement parking area and could be controlled by whomever was riding inside. It could go to the desired floor without stopping.

He then located an emergency fire door that entered the building at street level that was only thirty feet away from the elevator. He spent time researching and then checking out his ability to blind security cameras and open the emergency door without setting off any alarms.

He was then able to access the controls for the lock on Aldo's office door and the emergency call button that was at Aldo's desk.

There were two cameras in Aldo's office on each side of the room that panned the entire room.

Johnnie and the rest of the team spend almost a whole day watching what went on. They noted that Aldo spent much of his time on the phone with his various lieutenants checking on the field work of enforcement and collection. He also spent time with several financial managers checking on the money flow and the standing of the money collection from various businesses. They all agreed that Aldo spent too much time sitting and conducting what seemed to be a relatively boring type of work.

Alex commented that if she met Aldo at a party, his white beard, swept back white hair and his bifocal gold rimmed glasses made him look like one of her college professors. She would take him to be a friendly, amiable person with whom she could spend hours talking philosophy. He did not have the dark, sun-tanned look of what she envisioned an Italian mafioso would have. She added that he certainly did not have the vindictive appearance she had envisioned based on her recent experience.

Johnnie then suggested that they walk through how she and Trey would go to Chicago, he was not sure how they could disappear when they left the airport and then approach the mafia offices.

Johnnie walked them up to the emergency door and then timed their actions from the moment they opened the door and walked to the freight elevators, rode it up to the top floor, walked to Aldo's empty office and took up their position.

He said that he would put visual do loops in the security cameras so that they could sit and relax until Aldo returned to his office.  Then they would each stand in the two alcoves that had Greek statues in them.  Aldo's security should give him an OK and he would enter and sit down.  Then Alex and Trey would both make their appearance.  Aldo would most likely reach into his desk for his weapon, which would not be there but in Alex's hand.

She was to walk forward and offer it to him and explain that she was there to show him some magic.  She would ask him to access his bank accounts and see if they had the right amounts in them.  She then would show him a current account with zero dollars after she had done her magic.  The first showing would be the current amount and the second showing would be the accounts with zero dollars in them.

She would then ask him to look at his computer screen and she would show him pictures of all his relatives and bosses in Sicily and let him know that she had the ability to zero their bank accounts as well.

She would let him know that she had a life AP that monitored her heartbeat and if it stopped, all the bank accounts that he used and those of everyone he knew would go to zero dollars.

Johnnie pointed out that they would need to get the two guards that stood outside of the office to somehow be distracted so that a getaway could be executed.

Trevor suggested that the two guards be called into the office and be disarmed, Alex and Trey would then leave and lock the door so that no one could get out and the alarm to call for help would be kept disabled until Alex and Trey left the building and drove away.

They went through the entire scenario several times and fine-tuned each of the steps.

Alex called Harold Zimmerman of the Chicago area DEA and asked him if he would help her, and Trey leave the Airport unseen.

He laughed and asked if she would tell him why she wanted to leave unseen.

She gave him a quick explanation that caused him to readily agree if afterwards they could have a drink together so she could share the meeting with the Mafia chief with him.

She knew that he would take her to his aunts restaurant where they had done something similar before.  She asked him if he was acquainted with Andy Weller, the regional IRS leader and if so, she asked him to invite him to the luncheon because she would have a gift for him.

Harold said that they had done some business together and he would make sure that he would come to lunch with them.

He then let her know that he would meet her at the planes exit door and they would leave by the stairs that led to the ground.

Alex gave him the flight and the alias names she and Trey would be using to make the flight.

They left the next day on an early morning flight. Alex let Trey know that Johnnie had done a detailed search of the offshore bank accounts that she was planning to give to Andy Weller so he could arrest Aldo Viscuso on money laundering and tax evasion.

Trey laughed and said that he now understood why she was going to promise not to bother Aldo again if he would promise to stop trying to kill her. He would be in jail for money laundering.

Alex nodded and replied that he was not going to go Scot free after assigning a sniper to kill her.

Harold met them at the planes exit door and took them down to a black limousine and drove off. He introduced Tom, the driver who both of them had met before and said that they would drop them off outside of the mafia offices at the emergency entrance and then return to pick them up when Johnnie let them know that they were on the way down.

Both Alex and Trey had on and mikes and were listening to Johnnie.

Johnnie let them know that the entire team including the Chief were sitting in the huddle room following along.

They entered the building and walked over to the freight elevator and the door opened. After pressing six, both of them stood facing the elevator door hoping that the rest of the trip up would go undetected.

Johnnie suddenly commented that he was watching two guards just outside of the freight elevator walking the hallway in what appeared to be a security check. He said he would open the elevator doors as soon as they left the floor.

A few moments later the door opened, and they walked over to Aldo's office and entered. Alex went first to Aldo's desk, opened the right desk drawer, and took out a really powerful handgun that had three hundred grain bullets. She took it out and put in her pocket. She commented that she had fired a gun just like that at the firing range and it had a similar impact as a forty-five. The range master had commented that it was likely the most powerful handgun on the market. She checked the other desk drawers for any additional weapons but found none.

They each took one of the comfortable well cushioned, black leather covered chairs and waited.

The wait was a little nerve wracking, but they were counting on Johnnie's ability to monitor the movement outside of the office and give them an early warning.

A few moments later, Johnnie let them know that it was time to get into the alcoves and out of sight.

The door opened and two bodyguards entered, looked around and declared that all was clear.

Aldo entered, thanked them, and told them to go to the break area and relax because he was planning to spend the rest of the day making calls and checking on how the operation was running.

Alex smiled as she realized that Aldo had solved the one stumbling blocks of the operation by letting his guards go to the break area.

She heard Johnnie telling her that the break area was on the first floor.

He then said that it was time for her to do her part.

She stepped out form the alcove and said that it was really great to finally meet the person who had tried to have her killed. She watched as Aldo reached into his desk.

She took out his weapon and asked if he were looking for it and pushed it across the desk at him.

He looked at it and shook his head. Then asked her how she had been able to enter and remain undetected.

She said that she had a magician that worked magic for her.

She then said that she wanted to show him some of the magic that she could work that might convince him to stop trying to kill her. She then took him through the process of having the money in his bank accounts disappear and reappear. She asked him to call the bank of his choice and go online with them to check the amount of money in an account of his choice.

Aldo did as requested and was talking with them when the amount went suddenly to zero and as Alex said, "put it back" it went back to its original amount. He looked at her and asked how she could do that.

She smiled and reminded him that she had a magician working for her.

She then let him know about her heart Ap that monitored the beat of her heart and if it were to stop all of his accounts would go to zero. She then asked him to look at his screen and said that she was going to talk to him about his family, both families. His biological ones and his business ones. She commented that she knew where they all lived, where they banked and how much money each of them had in their accounts. They too would find their accounts zeroed out if her heart Ap stopped.

She added that she had friends on both sides of the law that wielded as much power as he. They were all willing to come to her aid when necessary.

She leaned in toward him and said that if he promised never to have someone try to kill her, she would promised to leave him and all his family and friends alone. She stepped back and asked him if he could make that promise.

He asked her why she was willing to make such a deal.

She looked at him and replied that she did not wish to kill another mafia head and get into a lifelong fight with his bosses in Italy.

He smiled and said that made perfect sense to him. He said that if she managed to get out of the building alive, he would make that promise.

Alex nodded and thanked him and then walked out of the office. She dropped all the bullets from Aldo's pistol on the carpeted floor as she walked to the elevator.

Johnnie let her know that he was going to keep everything in lock down until the end of Aldo's workday or when his guards returned from the break area. He added the entire team had a cheer they wanted to give her, and he put them all on loud as they shout out, "Great Job."

She and Trey made it back down to the emergency exit and got into the car awaiting them.

They were both looking forward to a great and relaxing lunch.

## *11 And Then there was Jail*

**H**arold led the way into his aunts restaurant and then went to the back private room.  He pointed at the head of the table and said that was where Alex should sit.

He asked Trey to take a seat to her right.

He said that lunch was going to be a surprise.

Harold's team members all entered and sat around the table.

A few moments later Alex watched as Jane Stradford entered and sat at the other end of the table.

Andy Weller came in next and sat to her right side.

A few moments later, to her surprise, Chief Johnson, Bill, Trevor, and Johnnie all entered and sat along the sides of the table.

The final two people to enter the room were her mother and father.

She smiled as she realized that someone had arranged the lunch and that she was about to get roasted.  She wondered how they had all been able to get to lunch to make it happen.

Harold said that they were all there to celebrate one of the most daring detectives that any of them had ever met.

Jane stood up and said that she had learned about Alex's mafia escapade from Chief Johnson and they both agreed that going into a mafia's boss headquarters without an army was as close to suicide as one could possibly get. And doing so and getting out alive was just short of a miracle. However, since they were all there to celebrate the accomplishment, it now looked like the work of a genius.

Alex gave a little laugh and replied that they were forgetting the fact that she had a magician that made it all seem simple, and they should be lauding him because he was the one that had made it possible. She was just the puppet whose strings he expertly helped to pull.

Trey nodded and said that without Johnnie's expertise neither of them would have dared to do what they had done. He went on to praise the work that Johnnie had done in identifying the three participants in the dental implant case and how he had helped track each of them down. He then highlighted how Johnnie had even had a finger in solving the love triangle case that had gone on in the dental office. Trey commented that Johnnie was truly a magician.

Alex walked over to where Johnnie was sitting and handed him the thumb drive. She said that she thought he should be the one that presented the airtight case of money laundering and tax evasion by a local mafia boss to the IRS.

She smiled and said that she had to keep her promise to that mafia boss of not taking any action against him but that did not mean that the IRS couldn't put him away for the next thirty years.

Lunch was served, toasts were made, and they were all chatting and enjoying the celebration when Johnnie said that he had arranged for John and Hanna to share the progress of the trials that were both in progress and Joe would share what the IRS was doing in the case against the dentist. He connect to a large video screen and Hanna said hello.

Hanna reported that Jason, who had attacked both Zia and Fiona, had received the maximum number of years in prison and would only be eligible for parole after forty years in prison with good conduct. She reported that he was led out of court screaming that he would get even, which indicated that his good behavior was starting out on the wrong foot.

John reported that Dr. Thronfield tried to make the point that there was nothing wrong with using alternative implants and that there was no law against it. When asked if he had informed his patients of the fact that he was using black market implants, he had replied that he did not need to do so. Six of his patients had testified that they had suffered from the inferior implants and had them removed by other dentists at their own personal cost and wanted restitution.

He shared that the jury had only taken an hour to return with a guilty verdict. The judge imposed a sentence of fifteen years and a financial penalty of three hundred thousand dollars.

Joe then came on and said that he was bringing charges of money laundering and not paying taxes against Dr. Thronfield that would most likely add another thirty years to his sentence.

He was also aware that a class action lawsuit had been filed against the doctor for thirty million dollars by all of the previous implant patients. He figured that by the time the government collected the delinquent taxes, and the implant patients collected their money the doctor would be broke. He said that he would have felt bad for the doctor's wife and children, but he learned that she was independently wealthy and would not suffer from the doctor's sins.

The Chief stood up, raised his glass, and said that all seemed to be ending on a high note on the right side of the law and on a low note on the other side of the law and that was all for which he could hope.

Jane gave an alternate toast saying that she only had star special investigators in her organization that always delivered superior results.

The Chief shook his head and reminded her that Alex was on his payroll full time and not hers.

They both clinked their glasses and sat down.

Rose-Anne stood up and said that she was told never to apologize for having gotten her daughter involved in an investigation of the Mafia and she had never done so.

However, every time Alex came home, she worried about her daughter and her daughter's work partner. Every time whether for vacation or for work, her daughter was either getting shot or shooting someone. This was the first time she had been home where she had done no shooting.

Russel stood up and said that he had built a special metal clad door that had served its purpose when the mafia had sent in two hit men to kill the family but who instead were killed by his daughter and her partner. Another time he had watched her have a dual with a mad racist where she got shot but still continued to pursue him. The racist only got away for a short duration until in another confrontation he met his fate at her hands. He smiled and said that his gentle lifelong fishing partner had matured into a gentle but deadly Cincinnati detective that always got her attacker.

Just as he finished, Matt walked into the room and asked if he was too late to have lunch.

Alex jumped up and ran to him, said that she was happy to see him and gave him a kiss. She asked if he had planned to stay and do some fishing.

He pointed to the door as Lindsey and Nolan walked in and said that he certainly had, and he figured that Trey would also enjoy a few days with a pole in his hands and helping Nolan with his pole.

Alex looked over at her father and asked him to arrange to take everyone out on the Golden Goose for another fishing trip to their favorite spot on the lake. **The End**

## *Preview of: The Nine Towers of Ku*

## *1 The Nine Towers*

The pine forest seemed to surround the valley's splendorous red, yellow, and lavender wildflowers and encapsulate the nine towered castle like, tan brick mansion that was at the center. The mansion sat on a thousand-acre plot. The driveway to the house ran for close to a mile from a small local highway. The isolation of the place was why Liam had purchased the property. It was exactly what he needed to do the style of recruiting that he had in mind. He knew that this place would allow him to operate freely and effectively.

He had been given a free hand at how he carried out his assignment and did not have to report his actions to Laticia, his sympathetic, softhearted boss. Soft hearted except when it came to following the rules and the adherence to lawful protocol. She was too by the book for him so he kept her in the dark as much as he could.

Liam did not have any of that sensitivity.  He was a patriot did what he needed to do to get things done.  He did what he thought was good for the Country.

He sat on the stone precipice and took in the nine towers where he had chained eighteen drug distributors.  It had taken him close to a year to carry out the task of getting the top distributors from nine major cities, so some of his guests had been chained in the house for a year.  He wished he could have moved faster but he had kept them well fed and encouraged them to exercise.

His goal was to either enroll them in the elimination of key international agents or to eliminate them and find the dealers from their regions that would.  The choice was to work for him or die. He had abducted his victims first on the west coast, then the east coast and finally down the middle of the country.  He had seventeen young males of various heritage, color, social standing, and he had one very good looking but very obstinate young lady that he was going to enjoy whether she agreed to his demands or not.  He smiled as he thought of her as the icing on the cake.

He had an additional top drug dealer from each coast and from St. Louis chained in the downstairs part of the house.  They enjoyed the comfort of the main downstairs bedrooms that were located around the base of eight of the towers.

This day, he had packed a picnic lunch and had hiked to where he was sitting so that he could contemplate the action that he would be taking over the next few days. The seclusion of the house had given him the luxury of not having to hurry but now it was time to take action in a methodical and swift manner.

He knew that he would enjoy the action and did not care how his recruits chose their fate. They were probably not aware of the price of saying no but that was what made it so exhilarating for him. He knew and that knowledge seemed to glow in his mind and excite his entire body.

One choice gave him a recruit that he had bent to serve him. That choice was less appealing to him than a rebellious no, but it was the choice he needed to carry out his mission.

The other choice gave him the same enjoyable taste equivalent to a box of top-quality Danish chocolates melting in his mouth, when he pulled the trigger of his forty-five and blew their faces off as the bullet put into the back of their skull exited in the middle of their face taking the soft jelly of their brains with it. It so excited him that he often had to suppress ejaculation.

Even sex was less exciting than pulling the trigger and enjoying the pattern made on the floor or the far wall. He always stood for a few minutes to take in the splendor of the red and white splatter.

The field of wildflowers surrounding the mansion seemed to augment the colors that were floating in his mind as he contemplated the coming few days and played various scenes in his head.

He knew that he would have a fair number of defiant noes and that often the second person having seen the result of a no would readily say yes.

Each day he would take the yeses and put them on flights back to their home towns with the first set of instructions that they were to carry out. He figured it would take him three days to empty the nine towers.

He contemplated all yesses from the top distribution leaders. They most likely would hear the gunshots that followed the noes, and they were in their positions because they knew how to negotiate, were more interested in living and to have a chance to money, they would make than in being defiant.

Once his recruiting was done it would take him a day to clean the place and get it ready for the next cycle of recruits. The recruitment would end when he had a sufficient number of distributors following his orders. Once they were all in place, he would focus their distribution to get the drugs flowing to the foreign agents he would target. The drugs would be both legitimate and illegitimate. He had doctors on his payroll that would provide him the legitimate drugs and he would have his recruits deliver those drugs but with the desired modification that would make them deadly.

He planned to carry out the elimination of the foreign agents in a swift and deadly manner.

He finished his lunch and went back to the house.

He entered via the back door that led into a grand kitchen that featured a hooded six burner gas stove at the center. A massive refrigerator with a black exterior that matched the black marble that embraced the gas stove stood directly behind it.

Stainless-Steel clad pots and pans of every design hung on the left side of the stove and a large set of nonstick utensils hung along the other side.

A set of twelve premier knives rested in their oak wood holder to the right of the stove. It was definitely a kitchen that had been designed for a chef.

He walked around the island to the refrigerator and helped himself to a beer. He gave a laugh as he thought about the fact that he had a huge supply of hot dogs and eggs but not much else. He fed boiled eggs and hot dogs to his captives. He also threw in an orange and apple per day for each of them. They did not go hungry, but they did not get meals prepared by a chef.

He grilled steaks, baked potatoes, and made salads for himself and his three most important recruits. He intended to gain their support both through coercion and also by feeding them well. He wanted them to understand that he was not trying to muscle them into submission.

They would have the same choice to make as those chained in the rooms above them, but he did not expect to shoot any of them. He expected them to be smart enough not to say no.

He put the water on for the hot dogs, took out the buns and condiments that were designated to the eighteen upstairs guests and added an apple for each.

The upstairs always got served first. That way he could focus on doing a good job with the four downstairs meals.

For his three downstairs guests and himself, he had the steaks marinating. He would dry fry them and then melt blue cheese over them. He had mashed potatoes to go with them as well as a large helping of asparagus spears. He would also provide each of them with a glass of beer.

He ate by himself. He did not want to have any social connection with any of them.

The next morning, he distributed the boiled eggs and an orange to the upstairs guests.

He prepared two over easy eggs and a large sausage patty for the downstairs breakfast.

This was the day that he would ask the crucial question to each of those that he held captive. He smiled as he thought about the fact that he was going to go by a FIFO order for all the people he had been holding in his human inventory.

He went upstairs and removed the breakfast dishes from each of the tower rooms.  Then he returned to the first room where he was holding Orson Ambrose and Sebastian Cassidy who were his Seattle captives.  He addressed them by their full names and told them it was time for them to choose to serve him or not.  He had them kneel and stood behind them.

He pulled out his forty-five and asked Orson whether he was willing to do as he would be instructed to do.

Orson told him he was a bastard and should go to hell.

Liam smiled and pulled the trigger and watched the mix of blood, brains, and hair spray across the room.  He stood for a long time enjoying the sight.  He knew what the answer he would get from Sebastian and wanted to enjoy the answer he had received from Orson.

He stepped behind Sebastian and asked the same question.

Sebastian shook his head up and down indicating that he would do as told.

Liam pushed a mop and bucket in front of him and told him to clean up the mess his partner had made.  He then pointed to a body bag that he carried into the room and told him to put his buddy into it and to clean the room.  He let him know that he would be released and get to go home that afternoon.

His next two captives were the two from L.A., Elisa Amos, and Mateo Garcia.  He went through the same routine.  He was surprised that Elisa and Mateo both agreed to follow his orders.

He had expected Elisa to say no to his request and had been prepared to take her to the bedroom before shooting her.  Instead, he felt somewhat relieved that she had said yes.  He had come to like her.  She had a survivor attitude.  He figured she would do well when she got back to L.A.

He informed the two of them that they would be returning to LA that afternoon.

His San Diego two, Thiago Bandello and Osvaldo Comonte ended up being a repeat of the first two.  He shot Thiago and after enjoying the moment, gave Osvaldo the job of cleaning up and putting his buddy in a body bag.

He went to the next set of rooms that held the six that he had abducted along the east coast.  Riggs Melville made the mistake of saying no.  His buddy, Rowan, was eager to say yes.

The two from New York were both agreeable to doing as they were told.

It turned out that the Miami two followed the no-yes pattern and Dante Cruz ended up in the body bag.

He then went from the two in New Orleans, the two in St. Louis and the two in Chicago and got all yeses.  He wondered if the shots from his forty-five had been heard by all those saying yes.  He decided in the future to use a silencer so that he could get an honest answer to his question.

He then went downstairs and had the three leaders kneel in front of him.  He asked the L.A. leader whether he would work with him to take out some bad international spies.  He got the agreement that he had expected.

He let him know that he would be driven to the airport with four young drug runners.  Two of whom were from L.A., one from Seattle and one from San Diego.  He suggested that they all chat and agree to work together.  They would all have first class tickets to L.A.

He did the same with the Miami leader and let him know that he would be flying out with four of the young drug runners.

He asked Mylo for his answer and then let him know that he would be leaving the grounds with six young distributors who seemed eager to be back in the field.

Unknown to Liam, a trespasser hunting rabbits and squirrels had been sitting almost in the same spot where he had lunch the day before.  This hunter had heard the shots and had called in the shootings.  The hunter was asked if he was sure about the shooting and that he should come to the station to put in a formal report.  The hunter thought about it and decided that he might get sued for trespassing and decided to go back to his car and go home.

## <u>2 The Occupants</u>

Orson could not remember a time in his life that he was not mad. His father had beaten him regularly for the smallest of excuses. His mother was a junky who was seldom coherent. He was often left on his own to feed himself whatever he could prepare. He ate lots of canned soups, peanut butter and jelly and salami sandwiches. He ran away from home at the age of twelve and never looked back.

He found home at a soup kitchen that let him work for some food and sleep in one of their cots that was available for the homeless. Then the soup kitchen closed, he was out on the street making his way as best he could. Dumpster diving was his main source of food.

He watched the drug pushers distributing and periodically getting into gun fights amongst themselves. Then one day the gunfight was all around him and one of the pushers died in his arms. Before dying he learned where his supplier could be found, he was also handed a roll of money to give to that supplier. It was more money than he had ever had.

It lasted him almost six months.

Then he went looking for the drug supplier. It wasn't hard to find him, but it was hard to convince him that he could be a good distributor and trusted to bring the cash back to him. He was given a high school as his distribution territory and was soon bringing in more money than had ever been produced there. He was rewarded by being assigned the local university where he had the same success. His final step up was to the central downtown area where he was just getting started when he was snatched off the street and put in the back of a panel truck into a cage.

His captor was a large dark-haired, bearded guy with piercing black eyes who simply said that he was going to be given the opportunity of a lifetime.

The real outcome was that he spent almost a year chained in a room with another Seatle drug distributor.

Sebastian had first met Orson in the Seattle city center where they were both distributing their drugs. They had territories adjacent to each other and agreed to cooperate and help each other. It turned out they had similar family experiences, so they related well to each other. To have ended up in the same cage in the back of a panel truck had been a surprise to both of them.

Orson was the angriest about having been kidnapped. Sebastian was upset but figured it did no good to get angry he wanted to get even. He wondered why and wondered what the reason might be for the kidnapping.

It had been almost a year and the only thing that he had gleaned during that time was that their kidnapper wanted he and Orson to become subservient to him. He knew that there were at least four more captives. Two he had learned were from the L.A. area and two were from San Diego. Elisa was the only female in the group, and she was a person that he would never want to have mad at him. And she was really mad at her abductor.

Elisa was not mad she was furious and was determined to take revenge on the person who had thrown her into a cage like an animal and then had kept her chained for close to a year. It was enough time that she had figured out how she would eventually repay her abductor. His size and capability would not prevent her from getting even. If he ever let her loose, she would wait until the moment he let his guard down. Then she would take him down and she would put him through much worse treatment that he was putting her through. She was no stranger to killing. She had buried both of her parents to repay them for their years of abuse. She had almost a year to examine various scenarios for her pay back and she kept adding tortures that she would inflict on him. If she managed to get him in her clutches, he would end his life blind, tongueless, earless and have no gentiles and he would be screaming as he died. Her pastime was visualizing each of the barbarous things she would do.

Mateo knew Elisa well and he knew not to get her mad. He had many a beer with her. He had been present when she was fondled by a drunk as they sat at the bar.

She had gone into action and had hit the guy in the throat and then when he fell to the floor, she had kicked him in the side of his head and stomped on his face. The EMT's had put him on a board and taken him to a local hospital where he remained for more than a month.

Elisa had ignored the entire process and had returned to nursing her beer as if nothing had happened.

He was surprised to find the two of them in the same cage in the back of a truck. Later and for almost a year, they had shared the same common area where they were chained by their ankles to two rings in the floor. He had listened to her describe all the things she planned to do to their capture. She had also warned him to agree to whatever conditions that they were given for their release. She said that saying no might be what got them killed.

Thiago had been walking along the broad walk enjoying the setting sun before going to distribute his wares when he felt a gun on his back and was told to walk into the parking lot where he was put into a cage in the back of a panel truck. He was surprised to see four other people in two other cages before the back doors were closed and everything went pitch black. He asked if he should start yelling. He heard a feminine voice advise him to keep quiet. He felt the truck moving and short time later it stopped. Not long after the back door opened, and a second person was put into the cage with him.

Osvaldo had been approached, shown a gun by the person standing in front of him and told that he should do as he was told or get shot. He figured he was being robbed and offered to give up the money he had. He had been told to keep it but to do as he was told. He had walked as directed to the back of a panel truck and had gotten in. He was put into a cage with a person who looked to be Mexican or from some Latin American area. He got in and said hi.

The doors were closed, and all was black and then the truck drove off. Several hours later the truck stopped, and the back doors were opened. Their abductor entered and introduced himself as a member of the CIA and let them know that they were being recruited and their cooperation would be the ticket for their release.

He then escorted them into the rest area bathroom and said that the next stop would be several hours away. He let them know that if they gave him any trouble, they would be left at the rest stop as a body for the police to find later. The ride lasted for two days and then they were taken into a house where they were separated two to a room and chained to rings that were in a central area between the two bedrooms. The central area was about ten by ten and had a table and two chairs.

A day after they had been chained, their capture came in with a cooler and said that it was a week's worth of food.

Osvaldo tried to figure out if he could get the chain off his ankle but realized that the clasp was held in place with a rod that had no key.

Riggs had just finished a bowl of fake lobster tail and spaghetti when a dark-haired guy sat down next to him and suggested that he accompany him out to the parking lot. He figured he was being robbed and wondered if he should try for his gun. But that idea was short lived, and he felt a gun pressed to his back and his thirty-eight lifted from the back of his pants. He was led to the back of a panel truck and told to get in. He took in the two other cages and figured that he was part of some drug distributor pick up scheme.

Not long after, the door opened again and a second person who he recognized as another distributor that he did not know personally but who had had seen on the street. He was put into the cage with him. He learned his name was Rowan.

Then there was a several-hour drive which had him wondering where they were going. A short time after the truck came to a stop, he found out from the person to be put into the next cage, Ezekiel, that they were in New York City. An eastern looking fellow was the next person put into the van. He introduced himself as Boaz and asked if anyone knew what was going on.

The drive that followed took them all the way down to Miami. It was a logistical nightmare of periodic stops at rest areas and eating take out from fast food restaurants. In Miami, the third cage was filled with a Dante Cruz and a Kenji Mochizuki. On the long drive that followed, the two of them shared the fact that they made most of their money during the spring break. They distributed so many drugs of every variety that the rest of the year seemed like vacation.

None of them had any clue where they were going but they all figured it had to be north. They talked and realized they were all drug distributors. All they had been told was that if they cooperated, they would live to do their country a big favor. The implied threat of saying no was very plain.

Dante and Kenji were the last to be taken from the panel truck and led into the house. Dante counted nine circular towers as he looked up at the house. He wondered who would build such a monstrosity. As he was being chained to the ring in the floor, he realized that he and Kenji would be sharing one of the towers. He wondered where in the country they were located.

The next day their kidnapper brought in a cooler and they were instructed to make the food last for the next week.

He listened to Kenji comment that his room had a bathroom and a shower. He made the point that it was a better place than the dive he had been living in, in Miami. He had to admit that he too had been living in a dive.

Ambrose was doing a booming business even though there was no parade currently underway in New Orleans. A large number of tourists were doing a crawl from bar to bar, and he was able to intercept them and almost do a continuous sell of his various drugs. He figured he was having one of his better evenings. Then a tall guy in a devil's mask stopped him and told him to walk with him. He was about to tell him where to go until he felt the gun poke him in the side. He was guided to a white panel truck and then put into a cage.

Not long after the back of the truck opened, and another person was put into the cage with him. For the few moments that there was light, he recognized his new cell partner was of Cajun origin. In the dark, he introduced himself and learned that his new partner was Enzo Beaufoy. He asked who the guy in the devil's masked was.

Ambrose said he had no clue, but he had interrupted one of his better distribution nights.

Enzo agreed and said that he was losing lots of sales.

The ride lasted for a long time and when he was given a bag with a burger and fries, he was able to learn from the ad on the bag that they had arrived in St. Louis.

He learned that the two put into the next cage were Zyair Smith and Lev Gataki. Zyair was black and a native of East St. Louis and Lev said he was from Russia.

It was another long ride with two meal breaks and bathroom stops at rest areas. Ambrose kept the conversation going as they rode along and said that he thought they were going north.

His direction was verified by the address on one of the ads on their fast-food meal bags. It was collaborated when the next two persons were put into the third cell.

Braylon Corbyn said he was from the Chicago area where he had grown up. Mykel Holmes said his family was from England, but he had grown up on the south side.

**Thank You for reading this far.**
To purchase the Nine Towers, go to:

www.remwriter95.net/

## **About the Author**

Ronald E. Mueller
remwriter95@gmail.com

Ron grew up in what is now Flint River State Park in Southeast Iowa. The 170-year-old house Ron lived in is built into a hillside. It faces a 125-foot-high cliff towering over the little Flint River. The house and the land talked to him about; the passing of time, the struggle to conquer the land, the struggles people faced and the wonder of nature.

He climbed the cliffs, crawled into the caves, dove from the swimming rock, collected clams from the bottom of the pond, gigged and skinned frogs for their legs. He trapped muskrats for fur, hunted raccoon in the dead of night, and with only a stick hunted rabbits in the dead of winter.

His young life was outdoors, and nature tested him.

He walked to a one room stone schoolhouse uphill both ways. A stern but warm-hearted teacher, Mrs. Henry was instrumental in shaping his character as she shepherded him from the fourth to the eighth grade.

It was a great way to grow up.

Ron graduated from Burlington, High School, went to Vietnam in the Navy. He graduated from The University of South Florida with a master's degree in engineering, worked for thirty eight years for Procter and Gamble, traveled around the world thirty times.

He has remained happily married for more than fifty years. His daughter and his two sons are all successful and his three grandchildren have all graduated.

His wife has humored and supported him as he became a full time professional story teller.

His experiences inter-twined with snippets of fantasy lend themselves to the adventures he leads the reader through.

### <u>Science Fiction</u>
**The Savitar Series:**
Journey's End
Savitar
Confluence
Savitar Series Collection

**The Door Series**
The Door
Aliens We
The Endless Hole
The Swarm
Esoteric Journey
The Gentle Eye
The Door Series Collection

**Bram Nielson Series**
The Fold
The Message
Fold Wormhole
Negative Fold
Ripples in Time
Bram Nielson Collection

### <u>Single Science Fiction Books:</u>
Current Past and Future
The Event
The Door
Viajante 7

<u>**Characters in the Story**</u>

| First | Middle | Last | Description |
|---|---|---|---|
| Alex | Cathy | Evercrest | Police Detective |
| Matthew | Timothy | Knolton | Alex's suitor |
| Rose-Anne | Germain | Evercrest | Alex's mother |
| Russel | Johnson | Evercrest | Alex's father |
| Helping Hands charity | | | Alex's nonprofit org |
| Trey | | McGregor | Alex's Detective Partner |
| Lindsey | | McGregor | Wife |
| Nolan | | McGregor | Son |
| Johnnie | | Smith | Old Viet Vet |
| Mary | | Higgins | Johnnie's Phili "friend" |
| Bruce | Lincoln | Johnson | Cinci Chief of Detectives |
| Mary-Anne | Leslie | Johnson | Chiefs Wife |
| Bill | Hamilton | Danson | Detective |
| Travis | Bailey | Carter | Detective |
| Dr. Rogers | | | Coroner |
| Jane | Elousie | Stradford | Lieutenant Governor |
| Felix | | | proprietor at fishing dock |
| Golden Goose | | | Name of the Yacht |
| Sandra | | Olson | Policewoman guard |
| Annie | Lorie | Scots | Missing girl |
| Linda | | Annies | older daughter |
| Lorie | | Annies | second daughter |
| Harold | | Zimmerman | Chicago DEA |
| James | Oscor | Kaizer | Sheriff of Wiggin |
| Abbie | Alisa | Bender | protect Alex married James |
| John | S. | Williams | Lawyer that was abused |
| Hanna | | Waverly | John's mate |
| Angelica | | | Angel on the hill |
| Brian | | Lexter | Cinci FBI Bureau Chief |
| Cais | | Leu | Alex's Viet friend |
| Tracy | | Hunter | Trey's Analyst |
| Chase | | Thornfield | Dentist doing inferior implants |
| Amelia | | Lockwood | Approves fact implant claims |
| Paul | | Elsher | Supplier of inferior implants and crowns |
| Luna | | | Dental office supervisor |
| Ezera | | Nightshade | Dental Hygienist recognizes sc |
| Dr. Mazerly | | | Previous owner of the practice |

| | | |
|---|---|---|
| Zia | | Dental Hygienist |
| Fiona | | Dental hygienist |
| Darcy | Barlowe | Patient that has a problem |
| Dr. Ava Whitlock | | Dentist that Darcy for 2nd opinion |
| Jason | Gravely | Vindictive ex of Fiona |
| Joe | Brown | the Cincinnati region IRS leader |
| Randolf | Task | Texas IRS agent |
| Andy | Weller, | the Chicago IRS leader |

Published by: Around the World Publishing LLC.

QR Links to

ATWP.US web site